Scholastique Mukasonga

Igifu

Translated from the French
by Jordan Stump

archipelago books

Archipelago Books
232 Third St. #a111
Brooklyn, NY 11215
www.archipelagobooks.org

Library of Congress Cataloging-in-Publication Data
available upon request

Distributed by Penguin Random House
www.penguinrandomhouse.com

Cover art: *penumbra 08* by Chioma Ebinama
Cover design by Zoe Guttenplan

This book was made possible by the New York State Council on the Arts with the
support of Governor Andrew M. Cuomo and the New York State Legislature.

This work received support from the French Ministry of Foreign Affairs
and the Cultural Services of the French Embassy in the United States
through their publishing assistance program.

Funding for this book was provided by
a grant from the Carl Lesnor Family Foundation.

Archipelago Books also gratefully acknowledges the generous support
of the National Endowment for the Arts, Lannan Foundation, the Centre National du
Livre, the Nimick Forbesway Foundation, and the New York City
Department of Cultural Affairs.

PRINTED IN THE UNITED STATES

Contents

Igifu

Igifu

You were a displaced little girl like me, sent off to Nyamata for being a Tutsi, so you knew just as I did the implacable enemy who lived deep inside us, the merciless overlord forever demanding a tribute we couldn't hope to scrape up, the implacable tormentor relentlessly gnawing at our bellies and dimming our eyes, you know who I'm talking about: Igifu, Hunger, given to us at birth like a cruel guardian angel . . . Igifu woke you long before the chattering birds announced the first light of dawn, he stretched out the blazing afternoon hours, he stayed at your side on the mat to bedevil your sleep. He was the heartless magician who conjured up lying mirages: the sight of a heap of steaming beans or a beautiful white ball of manioc paste, the glorious smell of the sauce on a huge dish of bananas, the sound of roast corn crackling over a charcoal fire, and then just when you were about to reach out for that mouthwatering food it would all dissolve like the mist on the swamp, and then you heard Igifu cackling deep in your stomach. Our parents – or rather our grandparents – knew how to keep Igifu quiet. Not that they were gluttons: for a Rwandan there's no greater sin. No, our parents had no fear of hunger because they had milk to feed Igifu, and Igifu lapped it up in delight and kept still, sated by all the cows of Rwanda. But our cows had been killed, and we'd been abandoned on the sterile soil of the Bugesera, Igifu's kingdom, and in my case Igifu led me to the gates of death. I don't hate him for that. In fact I'm sorry those gates didn't open, sorry I was pulled away from death's doorstep: the gates of death are so beautiful! All those lights!

I must have been five or six years old. This was in Mayange, in one of those sad little huts they forced the displaced people to live in. Papa had put up mud walls, carved out a field from the bush, cleared the undergrowth, dug up the stumps. Mama was watching for the first rain to come so she could plant seeds. Waiting for a faraway harvest to finally come, my parents worked in the sparse fields of the few local inhabitants, the Bageseras. My mother set off before dawn with my youngest brother on her back. He was lucky: Mama fed him from her breast. I always wondered how that emaciated body of hers could possibly make the milk that kept my brother full. As for Papa, when he wasn't working in somebody's field he went to the community center in Nyamata, on the chance that he might get some rice from the missionaries, which didn't happen often, or earn a few coins for salt by writing a letter or filling out a form for an illiterate policeman or local bigwig. My sister and I eagerly waited for them to come home, hoping they'd bring a few sweet potatoes or a handful of rice or beans for our dinner, the one meal of the day.

That morning, the clamoring birds in the brambles didn't wake me, and I never heard the piece of sheet metal that served as our door rattle as our parents went off looking for food. Maybe Igifu was drowsing that morning, but as soon as I stood up I knew he was there, I heard him grumble deep in my stomach, burrowing like a mole in its endless underground labyrinth.

I knew where to go to silence Igifu. As you know, it's bad luck for Rwandans to leave the house in the morning without first having something to eat. We call that *gusamura*. So at the foot of my parents' big bed there was a clay pot with a few pieces of leftover sweet potato, saved for us as always by Mama. Our arms were too short to reach the bottom, so she left the pot leaning to one side, propped on the neck of a broken jug. As I did every morning, I felt around for the two little pieces of sweet potato. They were stuck to the burned crust deep down in the pot, and when I tried to get hold of them they crumbled in my hand. I could only dig out a few little crumbs; I gave them to my little sister, who had come to join me. For myself there was nothing to do but scrape at the crust and lick the bitter brown paste off my fingers. I even thought of breaking

5

the pot to get at the coveted crust. But I knew how many long days of work my mother had done to get that pot from the Batwas. I chased that wicked thought from my mind. It could only have come from Igifu.

Every little Rwandan girl's first job in the morning is to sweep the house and the yard. Like me, you did that job without shirking. You probably liked raising little whirlwinds of dust in the yard, showing your mother and all the visiting neighbor women how hard you could work. But that morning I didn't have the strength for my daily chore. The bundle of fine grasses for sweeping the inside of the house seemed heavier than the big pestle Mama used to crush manioc in the mortar. And the opposite wall of our tiny hut seemed so far away I thought I'd never reach it. It's true that I took my time around the cooking hearth, hoping to glean a few grains of sorghum or rice that had fallen from my mother's wooden ladle. Following me on all fours, my little sister painstakingly searched through the sweepings I gathered together before I put them into the garbage basket. The harvest was not abundant.

For the yard there was another broom, made of twigs. I couldn't lift it, I could only drag it through the dust. The sun was climbing in the sky, turning hotter and hotter. That sun was no friend of mine, I knew. It kept Igifu awake, kept him groaning and ripping at my stomach with all his claws. Reaching the far end of the yard, I turned around and saw my sister lying next to her little basket. I didn't have the strength to carry her, so I pulled her up to her feet and we started back to the hut, clutching each other for support. Once we were inside, we lay down on my parents' bed.

I must have slept for a long time, because when I woke the sun was straight overhead. My little sister was still sleeping. Now and then she let out a weak moan. I put my hand on her chest, and I thought her heart was beating too fast, I thought I could feel it leaping! I had to find her something to eat. The banana grove Papa had just planted was too young to be harvested, but some of the trees were already budding, and inside the flower I hoped I might find a little *ubununuzwa,* the thick, sugary syrup we use as a substitute for honey. Alas, when I pulled apart the petals the heart of the flower was empty, and the bees buzzing all around, as disappointed as I was, took their fury out on me. I also knew of a bush at the edge of the field, just where the brambles start up, a bush whose branches were dotted with beautiful, bright-red berries. We'd long yearned for a taste of those berries, but Mama strictly forbade it: "I don't know anything about them, we never had them back home. They can only be poison. Don't touch them!" Needless to say, Igifu goaded me to disobey my mother's decree, and I convinced myself that only those forbidden fruits could save my little sister from certain death. So I hurried across the field and picked a handful of berries. I woke up my little sister, and together we ate my harvest. The berries were sweet, not very filling, but at least they weren't poison.

The afternoon dragged on and on. Occasionally I roused myself to go out and look at the sky. The sun was in no hurry to slide down to the horizon, and the big fig tree's shadow was too slow to lengthen. But every now and then the sky went dark and filled with sparks brighter than stars. Night wasn't falling: it was my vision going dim. Sometimes I thought I saw a shadow emerge from the thick veil of the brambles. Was that Mama, coming home with her bindle full of bananas and sweet potatoes? "Mama, Mama!" I shouted. But then the shadow vanished, and a cracking branch betrayed what must have been a fleeing gazelle.

The sun was sinking behind the brambles when I finally saw Mama coming, walking more slowly than usual, or so it seemed to me, with Igifu twisting and writhing in my stomach. My sister woke up and came running toward her, her in whom we'd placed all our hopes, crying "Mama! Mama!"

When she finally reached me, I saw that the torn piece of *pagne* she kept tied around the end of her hoe to hold the day's wages (a few sweet potatoes, some bananas, a handful of beans) was hanging empty and limp like the Rwandan flag in front of the local government offices. My mother saw me anxiously eyeing that rag, searching in vain for a promising bulge. "Well, I didn't get anything today, but tomorrow, they promised, tomorrow there'll be bananas . . . a big bunch of them." But in fact there was something after all in the folds of her bindle: little misshapen tubers, hairy and red with dirt. "These are *inanka*," said Mama. "I've seen the Bageseras eating them, I've seen them scratching around in the dirt to look for them. They spend so much time scratching that they've lost all their nails, and the tips of their fingers are as hard as hooves. I scratched in the dirt like they did, and I found these. I'm sure we can eat them too." Mama carefully washed the *inanka* (I think they were some sort of wild radish, that's what I was told later), saying over and over, "Now, don't you go telling people you've been eating *inanka*. It's no food for Tutsis. We never would have eaten *inanka* back in Rwanda. Especially don't tell the neighbors. I'll bet they've eaten them too, but they'd never say so." To set the example, Mama bit into one of the *inanka*. She closed her eyes. I tried to eat some too. They were hard, bitter, they stung my tongue. My little sister spit them out, crying. I don't think I could hold back my tears either.

"Go and sleep," said Mama, "that's the best thing you can do. I'll wake you up if Papa brings something home."

I must have dozed off for a while, but soon Igifu woke me. He'd dug a deep, dizzying hole in my stomach, like the big Rwabayanga quarry on the border with Burundi, where people said elephant carcasses and dead Tutsis were dumped. I felt myself being sucked into that abyss inside my body, and the walls of the hut spun like leaves in a whirlwind. I got up and struggled to reach the other room, where – like something from far away, from beyond the horizon, from another world – I could hear Mama's and Papa's voices. I didn't get far. I don't even know if I managed to tie on the little piece of cloth we use for a skirt so I wouldn't be stark naked in front of my mother and father. I collapsed to the ground. It was a slow, gentle fall, I remember, and it didn't hurt at all. That was when the lights began to shine. They seemed to be calling me from the end of a long, dark hallway, but no, it wasn't a hallway, it was like a tornado dragging me toward those lights, and they grew brighter and brighter and there were more and more of them, sparkling like the fireworks I later saw on our national holiday, but even more beautiful, and they didn't hurt your eyes, no, no, those lights didn't blind you, they were cool, they were soothing, and I went toward them, nothing could hold me back, I was floating, a wave of happiness pulled me toward the lights, the whirlwind went on and on but at the far end the light was waiting, I was sure it was waiting for me alone, I was so happy, and the colors! oh, so many colors, you'd need the colors of all the flowers on earth and words I don't know to describe them. I could see myself disappearing into that glittering spiral, and something pulled away from me, like a giant shadow freeing itself from my body, a twin, growing brighter and brighter, strong enough to push on toward that other light, to race forward . . .

I cried out . . .

I opened my eyes and saw my mother's face close to mine. She was holding me in her arms, saying, "Colomba, Colomba, come back, come back," in a gentle, lulling murmur.

"Mama, Mama, it was so beautiful!" I whispered.

"Don't talk," said Mama, again and again. She slipped a folded piece of banana leaf between my lips, and my mouth filled with a delicious, hot, sweet porridge that after a few swallows seemed to fill the hole Igifu had dug in my stomach. Much later, she told me how she and Papa had heard my cry and found me unconscious on the ground. They'd carried me to their bed. In spite of the shame it would bring her, Mama had gone to wake up the neighbors, the whole village, in the middle of the night. Together they'd filled a little basket with sorghum that Mama ground down to make the nourishing porridge that brought me back to life . . .

Sometimes I think about that light, but I never saw it again. I have only a very vague memory of blissful peace. Maybe that light was calling me, but I don't know who or what to. Or was it only a tempting mask put on by Nothingness? But why should death be so beautiful? And I think of those who fell to the machetes: was there a light waiting for them at the end of their torments? And then the memory of the light begins to hurt.

The Glorious Cow

I was seven years old, and proud as could be: I was my father's little cowherd boy. Every morning I woke with a start when I heard my father leave our hut, chiding myself for lying there fast asleep when I should have been outside before him, like my older brothers, out in the yard with the cows. I was convinced that my father never slept, that he always kept one eye open. No cattle thief would find my father napping. Cattle stealing was nothing short of a sport in Rwanda. The bandits were feared, but admired as well: their cunning was legendary. They had drugs to put everyone in an enclosure to sleep. Under the effect of their spells, the cows would silently follow them through the breech they'd made in the fence. They left no trace behind. They were powerful sorcerers, and they knew all the secret ways through the swamps to Burundi, where they sold the purloined cows and bought others. In Rwanda, some people's herds grew quickly. You didn't ask questions: it was too dangerous.

But my father knew how to ward off the cattle thieves' evil spells. He filled our hedge with talismans to protect the herd from any raid they might launch. What did I have to fear from anyone? Always within reach, just beside his bed, my father kept his staff and his spear – in those days every man had a spear, and he was never without it. Only later would the Belgians forbid them, to our deep humiliation. His bow and arrow hung by the door to the hut. Alongside my father – him armed with his spear and his bow and me with my little cowherd's staff – I was ready to face all the cattle thieves in Rwanda, and all their sorcery, but I was ashamed that every night I gave in to sleep and couldn't watch over the cows as he did.

Out in the main yard, my father didn't have to count off the cows: he could see they were all there with one glance. They were lying on the litters my mother and sisters had made for them the day before, while they were out grazing. My brothers set about getting them up. One tap of the staff and the lead cow would set the example for all the others. My father made sure none was hurt by another's horns as they jostled along, moving from cow to cow, his staff in the air, protecting the gentle ones from the hotheads (but he'd already burned off the points of the most aggressive ones' horns). He was the master here, and he had nothing to fear, not from the most ill-tempered beast. He worried over every cow that seemed slow to stand. He gave them a close examination, palpating them, prodding them, patting them, inspecting their ears, their eyes, their tongues. He studied their dung, its color, its volume, its consistency. He decided on the medicine they would need, and he pointed out the cows he thought too weak to go out to the pasture. Those would stay in the enclosure and be fed straw and fresh grasses we cut as we drove the herd home.

"Kalisa," said my father, "you look after Intamati."

I went straight to the cow my father had pointed out. She was what we call an *isine*, a cow with a gleaming black coat. My father must have assigned her to me because she was a particularly vigorous heifer, likely to someday become the leader of the herd. He probably thought Intamati was an auspicious choice for me, he must have hoped she would bring me good fortune. I knew what to do. I stroked her neck, murmuring her name: "Intamati, Intamati!" I carefully wiped off her dung stains with a handful of dew-damp grasses. I smoothed down her coat until it was silky and glistening. My efforts were repaid by a long spurt of urine – just what my father was waiting for. He always worried when a cow was slow to urinate. He would lift up her tail and bend in closer, imprudently, at the risk of being sprayed in the face if the stream finally came. No one would ever dare find that funny. In any case, isn't cow urine, *amaganga*, considered a powerful medicine? The morning's first warm urine is given to children with swollen bellies, a sure sign of stomach worms.

One of my brothers pulled away the barricade of intricately interlaced branches that closed off the main yard, while, on my father's order, the others guided and quieted the impatient herd. To get to the foreyard, they had to be led between the two bundles of bamboos that framed the enclosure's front gate. I followed close behind my ward Intamati, making sure she never gored another cow and was never gored herself, but that was all I had to do; she knew the way as well as I did. I admired her swaying walk, her long, perfectly curved horns, her big, dreamy eyes. She was my cow, Intamati, and she was my pride.

In the foreyard, not too close to the herd, we lit a big fire of damp grass so the smoke would drive away the flies that might otherwise pester the cows. This was the time to pick off their ticks and fleas, around their eyes, their ears, lifting their tails to hunt down every last parasite, searching their hooves for bothersome pebbles or painful thorns. If my father discovered a wound, he applied a pomade made from the pith of a banana-tree stem. And then we had the pleasure of smoothing their coats once again, murmuring words of pride and affection.

We led the cows a little beyond the foreyard to a fallow field where they could graze on the dew-swollen grass.

Then came the hour when the sun has climbed up in the sky but the early morning cool lingers on: *agasusuruko*, the ideal milking time.

My mother and sisters came to join us, bringing our milk jugs made from the wood of the erythrine, the beautiful red-flowered tree that watches over every enclosure in Rwanda. The youngest children sit beside the fire, each with their own jug, carved to fit their little hands.

Now the milking could begin. It was a solemn moment for all of us. There was a whole elaborate ceremony to milking, a little like the mass I now attend every morning, now that the cows are all gone. My father was the high priest, of course. He called the cows' names, one by one: "Songa! Songa!" Songa slowly came forward. He repeated her name, cajoled her with gentle words, called her "My beloved! My favorite!" We brought out her calf from the stable, led it into the foreyard. That calf too had been named at birth, and we greeted him with cries of "Rutamu! Rutamu!" It wasn't easy holding him back. As soon as we let go, he ran to his mother and began to nurse hungrily. Squatting under the cow, my father kept an eye on Rutamu's muzzle. As soon as it was spattered with a yellowish foam, we pulled him away from the udder and put the jug under the teat. It took all my older brother's strength to drag that poor calf away from his feast. We consoled him with a handful of reeds and the cooking water from a potful of beans; once the milking was done he would come back to his mother to lick off the last bits.

My father had hitched up his *pagne* and clasped the jug between his knees. He was a good milker. You can always tell a good milker by his gentle, regular rhythm. You can hear it by the *shyushyu! shyushyu!* of the milk spurting from the teat between his hands. Today, in Nyamata, I would give anything to hear that sound again.

The first cow to be milked was always the one that had just calved. She had the most milk to give, a very yellow milk, very rich, very thick. Only the youngest children got that milk. The milker hurried to fill their little jugs, and they drank it all straight down. But you mustn't take a jug of that precious milk just any old way. You had to sit down – no squatting – with your legs outstretched, your shoulders very straight. It was my mother who gave that milk to her children. "*Akira amata! Nyakugira amata!*" she murmured: "I give you this milk! May you always have milk!" The children took the milk, holding the jug in their two little hands – you always hold a milk jug with both hands, out of respect, out of reverence for the cow, so that she might live a long life. It was a little like the *abapadris* with their chalices, but the milk actually nourished us. The children drank it down in one go, never pausing for breath. With that a mother had nothing to fear: her children's good health was assured. It was a joy to see Mama contemplating her children's noses and cheeks spattered with light yellow foam, just like the calf. Once they'd emptied their jugs, the little ones held them out to my mother, their eyes shining with delight.

Bowed in veneration, my mother and sisters carried the milk jugs into the main hut. They set them down in their place of honor on the *uruhimbi*, the shelf that runs along the curve of the house's inner wall. An elaborate system of traps shielded it from rats, because if a rat fell into a jug it was less the spoiled milk that would be wept over than the curse it would inevitably bring to the family. The *uruhimbi* was like milk's altar, it was the family's pride and honor. The big milk jugs with their pointed lids protected us like the saints' statues in the church. What could we possibly have to fear? We had plenty of milk, the source of all life.

If man is master of the cows, woman is mistress of the milk. Before I was old enough to join my brothers tending the herd, I followed close behind my mother as she saw to her daily tasks, particularly the ones that involved milk. She poured the fresh morning milk that we hadn't drunk into a big neckless jug. On the *uruhimbi*, in other identical pots, the milk had been sitting for several days. Mama skimmed off the cream with a little wooden spoon, gradually filling a very black little jug, the *akabya*. Once there was enough, it was time to make butter. With great care and respect, my mother took down the churn, which hung over the *uruhimbi* in a net like a hammock. I saw the sun pass by before my eyes: that churn shone far brighter than the *abapadris'* monstrance on procession day. Because not just any gourd is fit to be a churn. Very few have the necessary qualities: hips like a young woman, as my mother said, and a neck like a black-crowned crane. Those curves had to be as soft to the touch as a baby's dimpled thigh. Water must never come near it: like the cow, it was cleaned with a tuft of *ishinge*, the soft, delicate grass that girls offered honored guests, and varnished with the very butter it mysteriously engendered within its flanks. My mother would sit down against the screen that hid my parents' big bed, her legs outstretched, her shoulders very straight, then lay the churn on her thighs and rock it back and forth like a baby. My little sisters and I looked on in fascination as the churn's belly rolled to and fro, wondering if it might bring forth not only the coveted butter but also the poor little orphan girls my mother had told us about, imprisoned inside it by their cruel stepmother.

Once the milking was done, we led the cows to the pasture. Houses and farmland hadn't yet taken over the countryside: there was still room for cows. Sometimes my father came with us, but most often he left the job of leading the herd to my big brother. There were many other things to be done. My father was an elder, the living memory of all the families on our hill and the others around it: he knew all the ancestors, all the bloodlines, genealogies, alliances, rivalries. People came to seek out his counsel. He knew how to disarm a conflict with a well-chosen proverb. The men gathered in the shadow of a big fig tree, on the grass of the field we call the *agacaca*, discussing the latest news from Nyanza, the royal palace, talking over the new ways the white people had come up with to deepen the misery of the Rwandans and their cows, but most importantly deciding who would be allotted what grazing land (which gave rise to arguments, bargains, and recriminations without end), and the order in which each herd would go to the drinking troughs to avoid crowding and scuffles as much among the animals as among the cowherds.

It's not good for the head of a family to stay home in his enclosure with his wife. Not that she would hear of it anyway: she would soon be an object of mockery for the neighbor women, who would mutter behind her back: "Her husband's like the family dog, always hanging around the house, *sumugabo n'imbwa*." A man's job is to defend the family's interests in the world outside. He's like a Minister of Foreign Affairs. And an important man like my father had to call on the chief, spend time in his house, take part in the evening gatherings, listen to what was said over the jugs of beer, offer cows, receive other cows in return. But the moment he could he came back to his herd.

The pastures lay on the steep slope of the hill, where there was no way to build an enclosure. Grazing land was scarce in the valleys, and the privileged people kept it all to themselves. In the rainy season – and you know what a long season that is in Rwanda – the cowherds huddled under their *isinde*. An *isinde* was a sort of portable shelter that you carried over you like a hood. It looked a little like the sentry box outside the Gako military camp, but the *isinde* was much lighter: it was woven from dried banana-tree leaves. We stored our *isinde* in a dry spot beneath a big rock. That was our hiding place, where we kept a supply of spare staffs, bows and arrows, flutes . . . And it was also where we stowed our meager provisions for the day.

Across the swamp, on the facing hillside, there were other cows and other cowherds. The custom was to trade insults back and forth – I won't repeat those insults here, they always involved someone's mother . . . And everyone sang the praises of their own cows, which were of course beyond all compare, and mocked their neighbor's. Meanwhile, some played the flute. They all made sure that the echo carried their insults, their praise, and their melodies as far as possible, but they always kept one eye on the cows, which had to be kept from grazing on poisonous plants or wandering onto steep slopes. For my part, I stayed close behind Intamati. My mother had given me a little pouch made of black and yellow banana leaves. That was for collecting my cow's manure, whose beautiful bright green had caught my mother's eye. "That's just what I need to seal the big sorghum and eleusine baskets at the foot of our bed," she told me. I diligently filled up my pouch and put it away in the hiding place, out of the sun.

When the day turned too hot, one of the cowherds brought the calves back to the stable. The poor things couldn't nurse, because their mothers' udders had been coated with white clay. It was in those hottest hours of the day that you had to be watchful. Thirst could drive the cows to bolt downhill to the swamp, not waiting for the cowherds to lead them to the troughs.

Because we weren't about to let our cows drink from that fetid swamp. We got their water from a spring, carrying it in wooden buckets that we emptied into clay troughs. We salted it with ash from burned swamp-grass.

All around us, that water attracted a good deal of covetous attention. You had to keep constant watch over the spring and the troughs. Fortunately, you could see them from most of the enclosures on our hill, and the alarm was sounded the moment any interloper came near. The cowherds snatched up their spears and staffs to drive off the intruder. The water we gave to our cows was thought to have miraculous properties. It was forbidden to boil or cook with it. That water protected us from illness, and most importantly from evil spells. I don't know if the little vial of Lourdes water that the *abapadris* gave me is as powerful.

Once they'd drunk their fill, the cows rested and ruminated in the shadow of a grove or on a hillside out of the sun. Is there a happier time for a cowherd than the moment when he can rest his staff on the back of his neck, fold his right leg against his left thigh, and tranquilly survey his herd?

The cows came back to the enclosure at nightfall, and then every evening was a celebration. The cowherds danced and improvised poems in their animals' honor. The lead cow's praises were sung. I always took care to gather the tenderest grasses for Intamati. Sometimes all the herds of everyone on the hill came together in a long, long parade – it was like being at the King's. The children clapped as the herds ambled by, and the women threw out their cries of joy. Then everyone collected his own cows, which could take time, but that forest of horns was a beautiful sight, one that all the men of the hill never tired of admiring.

The cowherds were hungry, but there were still the cows to be milked, with the same ceremony as that morning. Then we walked them into the main yard, where smoke was billowing from a fire of wet grass. The cows lay down on a carpet of fresh litter. As a last homage, we offered each one a handful of very green grass. The cowherds lined up by the door of the hut. I was hoping my mother would bring me my wooden plate filled with beans soaking in rancid butter, but *ibirunge*, my very favorite dish, was not to be eaten every evening. On the other hand, there was always a pot of whipped milk, *ikivuguto*, to dispel the cowherds' exhaustion and restore their strength. But even with that I was half-asleep on my feet, so I lay down on my mat in the entryway, next to the last-born calf, vowing that the next morning I'd be the first one up, before my brothers, before my father, and the first out with the cows.

——— ——— ———

Days when I didn't have school, my father Kalisa would come home from his daily mass and say to me: "Karekezi, you're a man now. Come with me, it's time you learned how to look after cows." There were no cows in Nyamata, of course, at least not among the Tutsis who'd been forced to resettle there, but my father spent his days leading his phantom cows into the fields of memory and regret.

"Look," he would tell me as we walked past the banana grove at the far end of the foreyard, so lovingly tended by my mother, the source of the bananas we children so loved, "look, your poor mother cares for her banana trees like they were her calves. Sorrow be upon us! I've seen her: she pours out the beans' cooking water at their feet, and she collects that beautiful rotting grass like she still had cows, and that's all she can do with it now: feed the banana trees!"

My father had laid his long cowherd's staff across his shoulders, his forearms draped over it. His perfectly white *pagne* revealed his long, straight legs, thin, with no bulge at the calf. He traded that *pagne* for a pair of old shorts and a tattered short-sleeved shirt only when he had a big job to do: clearing a new field, digging out stumps. But when the agronomists came to inspect our coffee plants, he tied on his whitest *pagne* and majestically leaned on his herdsman's staff. His gaze distant, his pipe in his mouth, he let the young experts recite their endless instructions, and finally answered: "Then you're not veterinarians?"

We took the dirt road that ran through the displaced people's village. My father seemed blind to it all: the row of identical huts, the square plots of the coffee plants the Belgians made us grow. He wasn't easy to keep up with. It was as if there were some vitally urgent matter he had to attend to and he had no time to lose. If I met up with a school friend, I only had time to say hello and kick the banana-leaf soccer ball back and forth with him a few times. "Come on," my father would say, "hurry now, you'll have plenty of time to talk with Juvénal in the schoolyard tomorrow. I've got something to show you."

If we met any girls bringing the water home from Lake Cyohoha, my father would grumble: "That's what they've done to us. Have you seen those calabashes they're carrying on their heads? Back home in Rwanda, those calabashes were our butter churns. No one would have dared fill them with water. Shame be upon us! And I know what your mother does, but it's no good, not even Ruganzu Ndori's water can replace the milk from our cows."

Mama always gave us water from the Rwakibirizi spring, which tradition said had appeared under the spear of King Ruganzu Ndori. That water had sprung up from the very origins of our people, and she hoped it would have the same virtues as milk. Which meant that we had to observe the same ritual: sit with our backs very straight, our legs outstretched, and drink it all down without pausing for breath. To my father, that was sacrilege: he who had never had a drink of wine would say, "It's like the *abapadris* putting beer in the chalice." But there was nothing he could do; he let Mama keep up her blasphemy. What milk could he bring us now? All the same, he was thankful that at least she didn't misuse the churns. If a gourd grew to the roundness that in Rwanda would have elevated it to the almost sacred rank of a butter churn, she didn't degrade it by using it to haul water from Lake Cyohoha; she put it on the shelf that stood in for the *uruhimbi* in our little square house, and would only entrust it – and only after a litany of cautions and instructions – to the one of us assigned to fetch that sacred Rwakibirizi water. Woe unto any water bearer who broke the gourd promoted to churn: that act of clumsiness could bring down the worst calamities on us. That curse had to be countered at once. My mother would recite the requisite formulas and sprinkle the family, the house, and everything around it with her purifying solutions.

The village had only one street, just an extension of the dirt road through the bush, and you couldn't walk along the row of little houses without passing by Nicodème's. Nicodème, the shame of the village! My father would make great a show of looking away to avoid any risk of witnessing the humiliating act Nicodème engaged in every morning and evening. Nicodème had given up on cows:

he had goats, he'd got them from the Bageseras. He was a clever one, that Nicodème: word had it he'd got them by striking up a friendship with a Mugesera by the name of Sekaganda. He'd even convinced him they came from the same bloodline. To seal that bond of kinship, Sekaganda had solemnly offered Nicodème his two finest goats. Every morning and evening, Nicodème would milk those two goats. Milking goats! What could be more shameful for a Tutsi? Hardship had dragged Nicodème into the depths of degradation. Everyone – under their breath, of course – called him Sehene, the Father of the Goats. And then there was the calabash Nicodème used to collect his goats' milk. That calabash had become an object of loathing and disgust for us all. We'd taken to calling it Igikorwa: the Untouchable. We were sure that cursed calabash would bring misfortune to all our cows, the ones we no longer had and the ones we might someday have again. There were those who thought of going and smashing that dreaded calabash under cover of darkness. But no one could bring themselves to commit such an offense. The calabash might seek vengeance and put a spell on you. Besides, who would have dared touch the Untouchable? A few of the women defended Nicodème, Mama among them. He had a frail, sickly child. It was for his sake that Nicodème had got those goats from the Bageseras and milked them for all to see despite the dishonor it brought him. The people at the Nyamata dispensary claimed goat's milk was healthy for children. This worried the men: would their own wives go off and get goats if their children fell ill? Everyone left Nicodème and his goats in peace, but they made it very clear that they wouldn't put up with those animals wandering at liberty through their fields. And once that was done no one ever spoke to him again.

At the far end of the village, toward Lake Cyohoha, you passed by Rukorera's abandoned lot. There were no coffee plants in front of the crumbling little house, but behind it a half-collapsed palisade of interlaced branches marked the boundary of a vast yard. Rukorera! A displaced Tutsi who had cows! Who for a time brought a little *joie de vivre* back to our village! They weren't our cows, of course, they were Rukorera's, but because we knew they were close by, because their smell – and, we thought, the smell of their milk – hung in the air, because the dirt road was peppered with fresh dung, it was as if a little bit of Rwanda had come to console us in our exile.

No one ever forgot the day Rukorera appeared among us. The sun wasn't yet up. We were awakened by a clamor we knew well but hadn't heard for so long. We were a little afraid to go see what was happening. Some wondered if an evil spirit had locked them up in a dream they would never escape, if that sound was the ghosts of the cows they'd allowed to be massacred now coming back to haunt them, or if it was soldiers playing a cruel trick on the poor cowless Tutsis. "Don't go," said my mother to Kalisa. "It might be buffalo. Or it might be soldiers' boots."

Finally the villagers opened their doors and crept out to the side of the road, hiding behind the coffee plants. Now there was no doubt: those were lowing cows we were hearing, their stamping hooves, the cowherds shouting out names we give only to cows! The cows had come back!

Soon followed by the women and children, the men set off in the direction of those miraculous sounds. At the very edge of the village were a few plots of land that had never been lived on. There were no houses, only the uprights of the steel frames the exiles were supposed to make habitable by putting up mud walls. But that morning, in the golden light of dawn, we saw real cows grazing on the sparse grass, four boys collecting dry wood, a man in a dusty *pagne* leaning on his staff, a woman unfolding the mat she must have used to transport the family's worldly possessions, and finally a little girl, lying on a bed of fine grass close by her mother.

The villagers stood motionless in the road, gaping in awe. The man who seemed to be the head of the family came toward us:

"My name is Rukorera. I come from Rwanda like you, from Kibirizi. We've had a very long trip. My cows are thirsty. Do you have any water I could give them?"

Water for his cows! Of course we would find water for his cows. Instantly, Rukorera had gained the esteem of us all. He was a real Tutsi: he thought of his cows before himself.

We had to give those cows a proper welcome, and offer them a drink worthy of them. Every available container was requisitioned, and all the children were sent straight off to Rwakibirizi, because obviously there was no question of giving those cows our stored-up rainwater.

And so Rukorera decided to stay in our village, along with his cows. "After all," he would say, "here we all understand each other, here we all love cows."

He told us his enclosure had been spared for some reason in the massacres of 1962. But it had to have been an oversight, which would soon be corrected. So Rukorera thought it best to disappear with his family and his cows before the killers came back to finish their work. He hid in the marshlands that stretch off to the Burundi border. Rukorera and his family lived on the animals they hunted and the milk from their cows. The long rainy season drove them out of the swamps. He'd heard that many Tutsis had been resettled in Nyamata; among them, he told himself, he would surely find a safe place for himself, his family, and his cows.

The whole village enthusiastically accepted Rukorera, and especially his cows. We helped him build a hut for his wife and his daughter, and another for his four sons, and then a stable for the calves. All the men wanted to help put together the fence. No one – not even my very pious father – raised an eyebrow when they discovered he didn't have a Christian name and so hadn't been baptized. No one minded – on the contrary, we all admired the heroic names he'd given his strapping sons, names that our poems give to the great warriors of old: Impangazamurego, He-who-is-armed-with-a-powerful-bow, Rugeramibungo, He-who-always-hits-his-target, Rutirukayimpunzi, He-who-never-flees, and Rwasabahizi, The-victor-of-victors.

The village felt alive again, and it lived by the rhythm of the cows. In the morning everyone gathered around Rukorera's enclosure to watch them wake up and be milked. We all happily inhaled the smoke of the big fire that kept the flies away. The women asked for a little of the cow's lovely hot urine, that precious vermifuge, and immediately administered it to the children. Everyone followed along as the herd walked through the village; there were often arguments over manure-gathering rights. The children scrambled for a chance to finally touch one of those cows that their parents were always going on about, that they themselves had never seen. Needless to say, everyone took Rukorera aside to bargain for milk. He was perfectly willing to swap some for sweet potatoes, beans, or bananas. But he only had ten cows, and they didn't give enough milk for everyone. And so it was decided that access to Rukorera's milk would be regulated. The elders decreed that priority would be given to pregnant women, young children, and old people. But rules or no rules, everyone knew they could always get a little extra for a few jugs of beer. The elders also came up with a schedule to determine when the cows would graze where, because everyone warmly invited Rukorera to bring his animals to their fallow fields, not only for the free fertilizer and the gift of a little milk, but simply because it was a pleasure to have cows so close by. Everyone was convinced it would bring their families good luck.

It was the evening milking that attracted the biggest crowd, women and children particularly. The young men wished they could get near the cows, touch their udders, but no one ever invited them to come forward, so they stayed away out of pride. Milking was a right reserved to Rukorera and his sons. They were very good milkers: we'd seen that at once, from the gentle, regular rhythm of the *shyushyu*. Rukorera's wife handed them a jug – those jugs were the treasure they'd rescued and brought with them in the mat – and once it was full she gave it to the waiting women, who sat side by side, very straight, legs outstretched, as propriety demanded. With infinite care each passed the jug on to her neighbor, not drinking, merely making a wish over that source of all life, a wish of abundance and prosperity for the family and the village. The last one in the row handed it to Rukorera's little daughter, who took it inside. It was hard going home after that, back to your little house where no rich milky smell was waiting to greet you.

But the mirage of Rwanda that Rukorera had created in our place of exile soon faded. One morning, the little crowd who came to watch the milking found the enclosure deserted. Rukorera, his family, and his cows had quietly moved on in the night. A great sadness came over us, but Rukorera's flight came as no surprise. We all knew he'd been threatened, we knew the soldiers had promised to come shoot down his cows. Later, we would learn that he'd driven his herd across the border and taken refuge in Burundi. He was lucky as always, Rukorera: he'd managed to save his cows!

Once we'd passed by Rukorera's lot, we turned away from the dirt road and into the thick bush. Kalisa fingered his rosary, murmuring one Ave Maria after another. But it was clear that his mind wasn't entirely on his prayers, because he regularly pointed his staff toward the plants and grasses he wanted me to cut. He examined them closely, chewed on a piece of leaf or the end of a stalk, and shook his head. "You see," he would say, "it's hard to find the plants cows need here. Not like back home, back in Rwanda. I'll have to ask the Bageseras, this is their land, but for Tutsis they really don't know how to look after cows . . . "

My father didn't approve of the way the Bageseras treated their cows. "Poor things," he would lament, "they're just bags of bones, easy targets for every sickness that comes along. That's the curse of the Bugesera. I can see why the King exiled deserters and rebels to this place: all you can do in the Bugesera is die a slow death, and I suppose that's just what we were meant to do. The Bageseras don't respect their cows, they let them mix with their goats, they're always using the staff, they don't even know them by sight. You've got to call a cow by her name, flatter her, whisper in her ear, sing her praises. And when you take her to see the chief, you drape her in flowers and beads. But when the Bageseras are out with their herds it makes you ashamed just to see them, they dress like the white people's house-boys, little shorts and a rag of a T-shirt, an *isengeri*. They don't even know how to tie on the cowherd's *pagne* – no surprise that their cows give so little milk. They don't know the proverb: *ushaka inka aryama nkazo*, a good cowherd lives by the rhythm of his cows.

But the Bageseras did have at least one quality that Kalisa had to recognize and respect: in that drought-stricken land, they knew how to make drinking troughs, *amaribas*. He'd seen them, and he always made sure we stopped by them. He dipped his rosary in the cows' water and mumbled a prayer that mingled praise for the cow with praise for the Virgin Mary.

Now we weren't far from our walk's destination. Fighting our way through the brush, we went down a hill to a little swamp. Even deep in the dry season, the soil in this valley was always moist. Kalisa leaned on his staff and gazed at the stagnant water. His eyes were fixed on something I couldn't see: "This is a fine place for cows," he would say. "The grass always grows thick and tender here. And there's water: we can make troughs. Don't ever tell anyone about this place. Especially not your mother – she'll come out to plant beans and sweet potatoes. This place is for our cows. Karekezi, you're my son, and this is a man's business, let it be our secret. When the cows come back, this is where I'll take ours. There's grass enough for them, they'll recover their strength for when we go back to Rwanda, because the road will be long and difficult, but we will go back, we Tutsis, along with our cows. I can see them all here, I know their names: Kirezi, Kagaju, Gatare, Mihigo, Rugina, Ndori, Rutamu . . . When the cows come back, that will be the sign: then it will be time to head home to Rwanda."

Finally my father tore himself away from his secret grasslands, where his phantom cows were already grazing. As we walked, he cut a few branches that might make good staffs. "You always need a few spares," he advised me. "You never know when a staff is going to break." Back home, he shaved off their bark, straightened them, sharpened the ends. Meanwhile, my mother weaved *intumwas*, churn-plugs, one after another, using only the banana leaves with the most beautiful tones of copper and bronze. The *intumwas* piled up, useless to us now, in a basket on the *uruhimbi*. No one was allowed to touch them.

We came back to the village at the hottest hour of the day, when back in Rwanda we would have been bringing the cows home. "Go gather some wood," my mother would soon order me, "it's almost time to start cooking the beans." And as I was out assembling a bundle of twigs I recited the lessons my teacher had assigned. Before long my father would go off again. He always had things to do, he said, at a neighbor's house, in Nyamata, at the mission, but I knew that most often he went back out to wander, leading his vanished cows with his staff.

When night came the men would gather in a circle under a massive fig tree, exchanging news, judging the imminence of the dangers threatening the community, looking for ways to ward them off, but once there were no more urgent matters to discuss the talk always came back to cows. Everyone had something to say about the cows he'd once had, and the cows he might have again. Someone would tell of the cow given him by the chief, and why not, maybe by the King himself! They described her coat, her horns, her personality, the calves she'd given, they recited poems in her honor. And the French words the teacher wanted me to learn, whose strange litany I repeated aloud, were now mingled with the exalted, familiar praise of the long-lost cows.

——— ——— ———

Like so many other Rwandan Tutsis, I eventually set off into exile. I kept up my studies for as long as I could. The stateless status given me by the passport issued to refugees by the High Commission didn't give me much chance of finding work. Loaded down with useless degrees, I was finally recruited by the Republic of Djibouti as a middle school teacher in a remote little town amid a chaos of black rocks. They raised a few camels, and their three out-of-place cows grazed on cardboard. I wept before that desolation: I had no idea that at the far end of exile lay the gates of hell. Through various covert channels, I managed to send my first paycheck to my father. In the letter that finally reached me after a long, roundabout journey, he told me – just as I thought he would – that he'd spent most of the money on a cow.

The genocide did not spare my father Kalisa, or my mother, or all my family, any more than the other Tutsis of Nyamata. I'll never know what name he gave his one cow. I don't want to know if the killers feasted on her.

I came back to Rwanda without even one cow to my name. I hope my father Kalisa wasn't too angry, in the land of the dead. I live in Kigali, in the Nyamirambo neighborhood. I teach in a private university. I'm married to a genocide widow. My first son already has a sister and a brother, my wife's surviving children. I share beer with my Hutu neighbor. He's my neighbor, that's all I want to know about him. I often dream of King Gihanga. The legend says that Gihanga was the first King of Rwanda, the one who brought cows to the country. And in my dreams, King Gihanga always asks the same question: "So, Tutsis, you were going to take care of the cows?" But I look away and I pretend I didn't hear.

Fear

In Nyamata, the displaced Tutsis' shadow, their true shadow, the shadow that never left them, that ignored the sun's course through the sky, that clung to them even deep in the night, was fear. And even today, so far from Rwanda, in this familiar boulevard whose storefronts and faces have taken on the tranquil patina of habit, it's still the same fear that makes me jump when I think I hear strange footsteps behind me, it's still the same fear that makes me hurry across the street to take refuge in the first shop I find, to go back the way I came, then turn down a street that will take me on a long, pointless detour. And if I spot my presumed pursuer's reflection in a shop window – a lady being dragged along by her dog, boisterous middle schoolers, a young man on roller skates zigzagging through the crowd – then I can laugh at the fear I feel in this city that's become my own, where no one, among all these busy people, would ever think of asking me where I come from, who I am, where no one, among all these people striding past, has ever for one second told himself he could or should kill me, and then I find myself studying those strangers' faces, because how can I be sure that one of them – that elegant, dark-suited African man, say – isn't there precisely to keep an eye on me, conspiring with others who will soon materialize and lead me into who knows what sort of trap, because he can tell who I am, where I come from, and when he gives me a smile because I must have been staring at him I hurry away, ashamed, cursing the fear that trails its long shadow behind me.

"In Nyamata," my mother used to say, "you must never forget: we're Inyenzi, we're cockroaches, snakes, vermin. Whenever you meet a soldier or a militiaman or a stranger, remember: he's planning to kill you, and he knows he will, one day or another, him or someone else. And if not today, then soon, in fact he's wondering why you're still alive at all. But he's not in a hurry. He knows you won't get away. He knows killing you is his duty. He thinks it's him or you. That's what he's been taught. That's what he hears on the radio. It's in all the songs he sings. He even wears a rosary around his neck so the *abapadris'* god will be with him when he comes to kill you. Never let down your guard. Don't believe anyone's kind words, even if he means them, because his plan to kill you is still coiled up deep in his heart. Keep your eyes open. Death is lurking everywhere, waiting for its chance. You have to be quicker than death, like the gazelle that flees at the slightest rustle in the tall grass. You have to admire the fly: it can see on every side at once. In front and behind, too. You need the eyes of the fly. Tell yourself you're a fly. And the dog: take the dog as your model. You think he's asleep, with his muzzle between his paws, so sound asleep that not even thunder could wake him. But let one leaf fall and he leaps to his feet! You have to learn to sleep like a dog. It's good to be afraid. Fear keeps us awake. Fear lets us hear what carefree people never do. You know what the *abapadris* say at catechism, how everyone has a guardian angel looking after them? Well, our guardian angel is fear."

There was the everyday fear, the fear we felt every minute. It walked with us on the road to school. That was where we could have used the eyes of the fly and the ears of the gazelle. The Gitagata girls who went to the big school in Nyamata all went off together. But they didn't talk, didn't laugh, didn't sing as all little girls do on the way to school, they didn't recite their lessons. They listened, they looked – in front of them and behind – up and down the dirt road, as far as they could see. If they heard an engine, if they saw a cloud of dust, then they dove into the brambles, huddled behind the greenery, hid their faces in their hands, they would have burrowed into the dirt if they could, like a snake in its hole, like a mole in its tunnels. The truck went by. The soldiers hadn't seen them, hadn't fired as they often did when they saw schoolchildren by the side of the road. They didn't always aim, they fired more or less blindly, or else they aimed at the ground beneath the children's feet. They only wanted to scare them, have a little fun. It made them laugh to see the terrified children scatter, staggering, falling, then getting up and limping on, jumping into the thorn bushes. And then, as the truck drove off, a soldier in the back might toss out a grenade that exploded in the middle of the road with a terrifying blast. Sometimes there were casualties. So we preferred to make a long detour instead of taking the road from the Gako camp to Nyamata. But we couldn't avoid going back to that road before we reached the first houses of Nyamata. So we ran, we ran. We were breathless when we got to the schoolyard. The principal was singing the national anthem, and we all joined in together, then headed into the classroom. We were entering another world, and we hoped fear might stay behind, outside the door.

But fear was still with us on the benches of the classroom. Félicien was a strict teacher. His long, flexible stick could suddenly dart away from the blackboard to lash the fingers of anyone talking or daydreaming. In unison, at the top of our lungs, we repeated the French words he'd written on the blackboard before we came in. We opened our mouths wide to show him our eagerness to learn, and also to be spared that vicious stick, so quick to encourage any laggard or drowser. From his podium, Félicien endlessly exhorted us to pay attention, we who were the most studious, best behaved children a teacher could ask for: "Everyone look at the blackboard, read the words after me so they'll sink into your little heads. If you look out the window, then the words will fly away, you can't hold them back, they'll disappear forever. Now, these French words aren't for Nyamata. Just keep them in your little heads, even if most of you have an empty jug for a head ('a leaky barrel,' he added in French). Maybe one or two of you will use all this someday, but the others . . . "

But we watched Félicien intently – taking care to be discreet about it, since you're not supposed to look a teacher in the eye – and we saw that at every opportunity, hoping we wouldn't notice, he anxiously peered out at the mission's big orchard, the nearby brush, all the unpredictable threats hiding out there. He kept a particularly close eye on the path that ran past the school buildings from the church to the market square, behind a curtain of eucalyptus. We seized that chance to glance toward the window, and immediately our fear erased all those French words we'd been droning so earnestly. Félicien was right: our heads were just empty jugs.

As if he'd been caught doing wrong, he hurriedly turned back to his blackboard and the lesson of the day. But his heart was no longer in it. His stick left us alone for minutes at a time. He couldn't stop looking out the window. He never once turned his back to it as he strolled among the desks, and sometimes, as if he'd forgotten his pupils existed, he stopped and stared at the empty schoolyard, at the orange and papaya trees in the missionaries' garden, at a little crowd of machete-carrying men on the path, coming home from their banana groves, at the dense greenery that hid the horizon. And until he finally went back to his podium, it seemed to us that fear had taken the teacher's place.

More than once, fear drove us out of the classroom. Félicien kept his eyes glued to the window. Again and again, he stepped out to consult with the teachers from the neighboring classrooms, who also sometimes came out to quietly seek his advice or warn him of some coming danger. We felt a little abandoned there on our benches, and we hurried to the window, trying like the teacher to make out where our killers would come from. We thought we could hear a sort of hum of voices from the orchard, we thought we could see the undergrowth in the bush shaking in a worrisome way, we were surprised to see no one out walking on the path. Finally Félicien would give us the order: "Come, children, we're going to pray." We left the classroom without a word, without a sound. The church was close by. But we didn't go in through the front, we went around back, to the little door of the sacristy. We sat shoulder to shoulder in the apse, behind the altar. There was no lock on the door. The teachers stood leaning against it, hoping they could keep it shut. The fear would fade a little. We were convinced nothing could happen to us in the church. I don't know how long we sat that way, not moving, not speaking. It was as if time had stopped. Somewhere between life and death. A missionary appeared in the church. He seemed a little surprised to see us behind the altar. Félicien and the other teachers talked with him for a time. He tried to persuade them the danger had passed, or had never been real. Finally Félicien and his colleagues were convinced. The *umupadri* headed out of the church first, through the sacristy door, while we followed behind, protected by his white cassock and the big rosary that hung against his chest. Once we were out in the schoolyard and sure there was no threat, Félicien would say, "My children, go home to your villages. Don't dawdle on the road. Run, run! That's what I've been trying so hard to teach you in gym class every day: to run. Jumping high won't do you any good, and it doesn't matter how nimble you are with a soccer ball: what you need to know is how to run. Even you girls, especially you girls who are so proud of your big bottoms, now you have to be faster than the gazelle. Run, run, that's the only thing that can save you." And we ran, we ran, as if to outrun the fear.

——— ——— ———

We mostly hid in the church when we hadn't quite recovered from a day of great fear. Those days of great fear! We didn't know why fear suddenly gripped the whole village. "They're coming! They're coming!" *They* meant the soldiers, the Party youth, the bands of pillagers and murderers who were always about to burst out of the mostly Hutu villages around us. Everyone's head filled with images from the 1959 or 1963 massacres: burned enclosures, cows shot dead, tall men "shortened" with slices to their tendons before they were finished off with machetes, women and children massacred to wipe out "the

race of snakes," rivers clogged with dead bodies . . . The slightest
rumor foretold the return of those horror-filled days: a minister's
speech heard by the teacher on the one radio in the village, the Party
cell leaders summoned to the town hall, a secret militant meeting in
the middle of the night, a convoy of army trucks on the Gako road,
arrests among the shopkeepers around the market square, beatings
of students home from school, ever more frequent and more violent
military raids on the displaced people's houses . . .

You always had to stay on your guard: any incident could be a prelude
to the final massacre, every word spoken by a high-placed official
could hide a coded call for murder.

The rumor had spread from house to house. "They're coming!
They're coming!" Soon we didn't know who or what had sounded
the alarm: Anselme coming home from the Nyamata market, the
teacher who listened to the news on the radio and talked it over
with the men in the evening, the children who thought they'd seen
soldiers in camouflage patrolling the bush. We knew what had to
be done, we didn't have to come up with a plan. We'd been through
this before. The watchmen hurried off to a place where they could
see the assailants from far away. Meanwhile, others put up flimsy
barricades, imaginary defenses where they hoped to hold off the
attackers long enough for the women and children to flee into the
bush, even if it cost them their own lives.

The women and children gathered at Athanase's as soon as the alarm was sounded. His house was the last one on the Lake Cyohoha side. The hope was that the killers would enter the village from the other end, the Nyamata side, leaving us time to hide in the brambles or the papyrus at the edge of the lake. For us children, those days of great fear were above all days of great excitement: nothing was the same as usual, everything was topsy-turvy! We were all together in the same house, Athanase's house! The schoolchildren didn't go off to class, the girls were excused from their chores, we didn't have to fetch water (we laughed to see the men heading for the lake with our calabashes). We were all one big family, with many children and many mamas!

The mamas were all with us in Athanase's back courtyard, even Mukanyonga, the pagan, ordinarily shunned by all. Everyone had come with provisions. We would never have thought there were so many things to eat in Gitagata, where no one could remember having a full stomach, and so many good things: perfect beans, *igisukari* bananas, white, mealy *gahungezi* sweet potatoes (which back home in Rwanda were never served without milk), even peanuts! All those things our mothers set aside to sell at the market – because we have to buy salt, said Mama, and oil for the lamp, and fabric for our school uniforms, not to mention saving up what we could for rainless days. And now the mamas were cooking up all those forbidden foods in Athanase's back courtyard and serving them to us in overflowing

calabashes – and it was Margarita, Margarita who was widely suspected of being a poisoner, Margarita who we weren't allowed to
ask for water, it was Margarita watching over the beans! "Eat, eat,"
the cooks insisted, "we can't leave anything for them, and we might
soon have a long way to walk with nothing in our stomachs." But
our stomachs had got used to famine, and all too soon refused to let
the feasting go on.

The mamas were like the hen that gathers her chicks under her
wings the moment she spots Sakabaka the vulture. Alas, we couldn't
shelter beneath their *pagnes*, but they did all they could to outwit
our fear. They invented things for us to do, since we couldn't run
or kick the ball back and forth on the road or play hide-and-seek in
the sorghum. "Study your lessons," they would say to the children
who went to school. We opened the treasured notebooks we always
kept with us. But we couldn't lose ourselves in our work. We began
to hate those foreign words, to suspect them of having some vague
connection with the misery hanging over us. The big girls who'd set
out to weave baskets soon lost heart and gave up. The mamas came
up with games for the littlest ones. They had them make dolls out
of sorghum, they showed them how to shape little platters for their
straw-and-twig figures to eat from. We asked riddles, but only in a
whisper, as if we were trading secrets. And that was what frightened
us most, because all of this happened in silence: the mothers forbade

us to speak out loud, and at the slightest sound everything came to a stop, frozen in awful anticipation.

Night fell. The watchmen and scouts hadn't seen anything out of the ordinary. But there was no question of going home. Our enemies were probably waiting to launch their attack in the dark. The men's vigilance doubled. They came into Athanase's back courtyard for a little food and rest, then went off again when their turn came to keep watch.

The children settled in to sleep in the little house, squeezed all together, which brought us some comfort. There weren't enough mats for us all, so the oldest ones slept on the floor. But the strangest thing was that we slept fully clothed. The mamas had told us: "Whatever you do, don't get undressed!" That morning, they'd had us put on our finest things, our Sunday mass clothes. They had the school-children put on their uniforms. And the women too had dressed in their fanciest *pagnes*, bought at the price of many privations, worn with pride on wedding days. Maybe they hoped they could still save all that if they had to flee, all those humble belongings, their most prized possessions. But more than anything I believe their concern for elegance was an act of defiance against the killers and against death.

It wasn't easy falling asleep. We were all listening for noises, the men in the back courtyard, footfalls on the dirt road. "You think they're going to come?" the girls asked each other over and over. Finally, just as the night was ending, sleep overcame us, but only to plunge us into a whirlwind of nightmares: it was a deliverance to wake up.

When dawn came, we were greatly surprised to find ourselves lying fully clothed side by side. The women were already at work in the back courtyard. There was no one to stop us from running out to the dirt road. We found the village and all its houses still there, no different from what they were the day before. We still suspected our persecutors of trying to trick us. We didn't dare go any further, out to the empty houses. But little by little came reassuring news. A few of the men had ventured as far as Nyamata. They'd seen no soldiers or militiamen on the road. The Nyamata market was bustling as always. At noon, the alarm was lifted. The days ahead would be hard, because we'd used up all our provisions to face the great fear. Now we would go back to a life lived on borrowed time, back to the everyday fear. They hadn't come this time, but we knew one day they would.

The Curse of Beauty

It was a terrible curse to be beautiful. For a Tutsi woman in Rwanda, there was no greater sorrow than beauty. And Helena was beyond question the most beautiful of them all, and her beauty was the bane and the torment of her sad life.

Helena was already the talk of the village when I was in primary school. She lived just a few kilometers away from us, but high above, on the ridge overlooking the Kanyaru, at the end of a dirt road, or more exactly a very faint trail, in Kirarambogo, the edge of the known world. My mother said her family and ours were vaguely related, and now and then we called on each other. Helena had been admitted to Notre-Dame-de-Cîteaux high school in Kigali, the best in all Rwanda, attended by the daughters of ministers, government officials, and rich merchants. I don't know if her beauty had anything to do with that.

I saw Helena in her glory days, when she came home for vacation at the start of the dry season. I would wait for her by the dirt road with my brothers and sisters, my mother, and all the local ladies, even some from far away who'd made a special detour on their way to the market, their bunches of bananas or baskets of beans sitting on the ground in front of them. The men were also discreetly watching, I'm sure, through the holes in the palisades around their enclosures, waiting for a glimpse of that peerless beauty.

To hear the village women tell it, Helena was in every way a queen – in any case, the cortege that accompanied her was worthy of a president, or a minister at least. She was announced by a cloud of golden dust, along with a riot of music and song. And then, at last, there she was. A veritable orchestra preceded and followed her: who knows how many guitarists, three accordion players, singers, poets declaiming her praises. A ten-year-old boy bore her cardboard suitcase on his head, while another of the same age carried her notebooks and a few schoolbooks bound up with sisal. Helena smiled a dazzling white smile, but what most astonished us was the extraordinary scarlet of her lips. She was dressed in a high school girl's gray, shapeless uniform, which nonetheless seemed to bring out all the perfections of her body. No one understood how she could possibly walk on shoes as tall and delicate as the legs of a black-crowned crane.

One day – I must have been in my last year of primary school – she gave me a nod: "Asumpta, you're a big girl now, come with us." I looked at my mother, who hesitated to give me her permission, clearly reluctant to see me go off with what she must have thought a wild crowd, but neither did she want to refuse the honor of such a celebrity inviting her daughter for all to see. "You can go as far as Kirarambogo," she told me, "but no further, and then you come straight home."

I immediately joined the parade, whose numbers swelled as we went. In the little village of Kirarambogo, women bearing jugs of beer joined our ranks. Helena had drawn me to her and put her arm around my shoulders. And then, for the first time in my life, I disobeyed my mother. Instead of turning back there, I went on following the path at Helena's side. It was as if the poets' panegyrics, the music of the guitars and accordions, as if all that were also meant for me, just a little, and so I made my entrance into the great yard of Helena's enclosure proudly pressed to her hip.

Helena's mother welcomed her on the front step of the mud-and-thatch house. They gave each other a long embrace, in the Rwandan style. "Come with me," Helena whispered in my ear. I followed her inside. I was astonished to learn that she slept all alone, in a room just for her: "This is my bedroom," she said proudly. "No one sleeps here but me, not even when I'm away."

The little porters set their loads down on the bed. Helena hurried to open the suitcase and said to me, "Look!" It was a veritable treasure chest: I'd never seen so many dresses, skirts, bras, lacy panties. And above all I was fascinated by a cardboard box full of those little sticks that paint your lips bright red and those tubes of Venus de Milo brand cream that make your skin so light – not the Kenyan stuff you can buy at the market but the almost impossible-to-find real thing, stamped *Made in Nigeria*. "I've got to pick out a dress," she said. "I have to be beautiful for all the friends who walked me home." She laid out three dresses on the bed and handed me a little mirror in which she tried to judge the effect of each dress she put on. It wasn't easy. The mirror was small, and for all her contortions and commands, which I followed as best I could, she could never glimpse anything more than a tiny bit of herself at a time. She finally decided on a long, bright-yellow dress with a print of pretty bouquets. "Hurry and button me up," she said impatiently, "they're all waiting."

The crowd of admirers was indeed eagerly awaiting her in the yard. The moment she appeared, in a dress like only the white women in Kigali wear, the guitars and accordions poured out their wonderment in frenetic rhythm. Helena bought every one of the jugs of beer brought by the women, along with – the height of extravagance! –

the peanuts sold by the children who'd slipped into the procession. Everything was ready for the *gitaramo*, the party. We all sat down in a circle, passed around the jugs of beer, and all the while the musicians, singers, and poets celebrated Helena's beauty, as she graciously joined in the young girls' dances. The festivities went on and on, I could scarcely keep my eyes open. I ended up falling asleep. The pain of a violent thwack to my bottom woke me with a start. It was my father, armed with this staff: he'd come out to look for me in the dark, and already he was dragging me after him like a goat.

——— ——— ———

Later, when I too started at Notre-Dame-de-Cîteaux (and it certainly wasn't my beauty that got me in, only an incomprehensible caprice of the quota system that assigned Tutsis just ten percent of the places in secondary school), people were still talking about Helena and her onerous beauty. The older girls who'd known her kept her legend alive. Still envious, they told again and again of the small favors and great privileges she'd enjoyed. They made obscure, winking allusions to mysterious protectors, the ever-changing "uncles" who waited for her in their big cars on Sunday afternoons. If she came back late (which she most often did), the sister on watch pretended not to have seen, or accepted her most outlandish excuses. The girls were also indignant that she alone had the beauty creams so rigorously forbidden by the school's austere regulations, that she alone straightened her hair, a fashion the nuns considered an affront to propriety. Needless to say, they'd noticed that the teachers – white men all – called on her more often than the others, spoke to her more gently, approved of her most inept answers. They remembered a young math teacher who couldn't seem to take his eyes of her as she stood at the blackboard and under his dictation elegantly wrote out the lessons to study or exercises to complete. "A true Tutsi beauty," they'd heard him whisper in the hallway, with an admiring sigh. Some even claimed he gave her private lessons in the little office near the Mother Superior's, sometimes used as a confessional by the school chaplain. The ministers' daughters wondered if they should tell the Mother Superior on her. No one knew why that didn't happen.

How much of all this was true? I have a feeling their scandalized portrait of Helena was in fact only the expression of their own endless frustrations.

———— ———— ————

"But if you want to see Helena," Gaudencia told me, "it's not hard. Just go to the Muhima neighborhood, you'll see a big shop, like the Greeks have. You can't miss her, she's right there in the window . . ."

Built on a steep slope, Muhima had long been only a muddy labyrinth of shanties made of clay, planks, and cardboard, but those hovels were gradually giving way to brick houses with sheet-metal or tile roofs, home to workers for businesses or foreign NGOs. The store where I would find Helena was a big concrete building, proudly displaying a sign painted in big red letters and four languages: MABOKO'S STORE ITEKA BIENVENUE KARIBU WELCOME. A wide covered terrace was piled with bags of rice or beans, mounds of fat Ruhengeri potatoes, cases of Fanta, Primus beer, Coca-Cola, barrels of palm oil . . . Inside, behind a long counter whose gate opened only to a handful of regulars, everything a Rwandan could imagine in the way of desirable goods was stacked high. And there, above the pyramids of Nido brand powdered milk cartons, above a dense forest of rolled oilcloth, black columns of tires, bundles of hoes, picks, machetes, in a sort of glassed-in watchtower, draped in a *pagne* whose leafy pattern bore the president's portrait like an enormous fruit, ringed with the motto of the republic, I saw Helena, whose stiff, straightened hair made me think of a papier-mâché mask, and whose lips bore a fixed smile aimed toward the front door.

She sat at a little table meant to look like a bookkeeper's desk, but instead of ledgers and invoices there were only Coke bottles, three of them empty and a fourth half-full. There was no staircase from the shop to the glass cage, which was connected to the upper floor only by a narrow catwalk. Helena sat as still as the statue of the Virgin Mary in church. I didn't dare greet her with a nod, much less call out to her, and when a clerk asked what I wanted I lowered my eyes, turned around, and once I was out the door fled as fast as my legs could take me.

——— ——— ———

Everyone knows everything that goes on in Rwanda – we might as well all be neighbors. And if they don't know, there's always someone to invent what they should. So people could tell you all sorts of tales about Helena, and I didn't need a Gaudencia to know about her life: the rumors were enough, even if the stories sometimes conflicted. Still, on one point they always agreed: Helena would never find a husband. Who could possibly marry her? Not a Tutsi, of course: the poor man couldn't possibly scrape up the dowry demanded by such beauty, and especially by Helena's parents, who were depending on their daughter to provide for them in their old age. And then on top of that how could he hope to pay for the clothes and cosmetics Helena couldn't live without? But could a Hutu take as his legal wedded wife a beauty who incarnated all the characteristics the white people attribute to the Tutsis? It would be a flagrant betrayal of his people. The authorities would never allow it. And so everyone agreed on the fate that awaited her: she would be the mistress of a rich and powerful man (because of course you can't have one without the other), getting on in years, who crammed his stomach behind the wheel of a Mercedes, who would show her off as proof of his success and unflagging virility – she would be one of those women we delicately called a "second office."

Still, in the beginning Helena worked hard to escape the unenviable fate of the "second office," because we know how those sad concubines end up when their beauty fades and their masters tire of them: in some distant neighborhood, or better yet on some faraway hill, their one-time lover builds them a hut where they languish their lives away, gnawed at by remorse, surrounded by their bastard children and universal disdain, reduced to selling bottles of Primus instead of their broken-down bodies.

Like many Tutsi girls, Helena found work as a secretary in a Belgian-run import-export firm. White people were always happy to hire Tutsis, girls especially. And for those girls – at least those with a little education and an appealing physique – that was one of the very few job opportunities they had, administration and teaching being more or less closed to them. The white people weren't particularly picky about skills, and some of them – not many – asked nothing more of them than the secretarial work they'd been hired to do.

Helena quickly learned to type and sort mail and bring that mail each morning to the director, Monsieur van Kloppersdyck, who devoured her with his eyes as she held out his letters with the kind of graceful gesture we learn from our dances. Any pretext would do for Monsieur van Kloppersdyck to call Helena into his office. Letters to be typed and papers to be filed were no longer enough for him:

his daily intake of coffee soared, thanks to which he had the pleasure of seeing his secretary set the cup on the desk very close to him, and then of gazing on her with delectation as she bent down just centimeters away from his shoulder to stir it with the little spoon until the sugar dissolved. But Monsieur van Kloppersdyck was a great family man, and every Sunday he sat in the first row at the cathedral. He confined himself to occasionally brushing up against Helena, or now and then giving her a quick, discreet touch after making very sure no colleague was there to witness gestures that he himself must have later thought wrong. He would probably have succumbed to the temptation in the end had he not, to his great disappointment and perhaps even greater relief, been obliged to send poor Helena away.

Because a wave of protests had spread through every cell of the Party; passed on by the ministers' wives, it soon reached the ears of the government. Intolerable things were going on, especially in Kigali. What good had the glorious social revolution done? The snakes were still there, or rather their daughters, tempting, perverse she-snakes insinuating themselves into the white people's society, usurping coveted places that rightly belonged to the real Rwandans, and their pillow talk spread lies aimed at destabilizing the republic. It was high time something was done. The quota system would have to be expanded, applied to every sphere of employment, white-owned companies first of all. And should anyone resist, the customs officials could easily find obscure administrative reasons to hold up the merchandise they were expecting, or uncover long-forgotten back taxes. If all else failed, there was always the threat of expulsion for moral turpitude. Obviously there was nothing Monsieur van Kloppersdyck could do in the face of blackmail like that.

——— ——— ———

How did Helena become Maboko's "second office"? What did he promise her that she let herself be exhibited like a trophy conquered at the price of a heroic struggle? We had no idea. It must be said that Maboko – Maboko Jean de Dieu – was nothing short of a legend in Kigali! He didn't look the part: a pudgy little man whose stomach had swelled as his wealth increased. Even if we found him ridiculous, we feared those eyes of his, lying in wait amid the fatty bulges of his face, shining with a fearsome ardor whenever the talk turned to business and money. Everyone remembered that he'd come from Gitarama, abandoning his wife, his two children, and a vague charcoal commerce. He never missed a chance to mention that he was born on the same hill as the president. He who could scarcely read and write, that was his calling card, those were the magic words that opened every door.

His beginnings in the capital were modest. He opened a shop in the Muhima neighborhood, where he later built his department store, once he'd bought up all the surrounding lots one by one. He gave that little shop a bright-red coat of paint and hung up a sign: CHEZ MABOKO, *credit offered tomorrow.* He drew attention to himself with manners that the city folk thought deplorably rustic. He spent his days sitting in a wicker rocking chair in front of his shop, on a terrace with a sheet-metal awning we call a *barza.* Everything that Rwandan standards of decency dictate should be done in the strictest privacy he did right out in public. Early in the morning, before a little crowd of gawking children, he savored his tea and fritters. At noon, a little servant boy set up a folding table and covered it with an embroidered cloth from distant China, then brought out a platter of goat brochettes, dishes of bananas and beans bathed in a gleaming, copper-red sauce, and – an unheard-of luxury – an entire can of Kraft cheese spread. The mothers came running to tear their children away from that shameful spectacle: a man eating, yes a man, shamelessly eating for all to see, brandishing a brochette in his left hand, and in his right an overflowing spoon that dripped onto his floral-print shirt, leaving long, dull-red streaks! But then just before sunset the same little crowd – now with a few of the parents mixed in – gathered again before the *barza* to witness the washing of Maboko's feet.

There was a complex ceremony to Maboko's daily foot-washing. The little spectators knew the ritual well, and they pointed out every divergence and misstep with laughter and shouts. They waited impatiently for the houseboy to appear on the *barza* with a bowl of steaming water, a towel draped over his shoulder. He gingerly set down the basin between Maboko's feet, then squatted to take off Maboko's sandals and carefully place them out of range of wayward splashes. He rolled Maboko's pant legs up to the top of his calves and waited, still squatting, as his boss tested the temperature with his toes and then suddenly plunged both feet into the basin with a blissful sigh. Maboko closed his eyes, sat motionless for a long moment, then gave the boy a sign. With that the boy knelt to take his boss's feet on his knees and began a vigorous massage, not forgetting to run his index finger between the toes, after which he dried each foot off with the towel. But it was the last operation that most roused the spectators' interest and curiosity: Maboko put his feet on the folding table from lunch and handed the little servant a round can, like for shoe polish, filled with some kind of thick cream. The groom (as Maboko called his servant) generously slathered his master's feet, which soon glistened like two fat sweet potatoes imbibed with palm oil. This caused a great deal of talk: what could that mysterious unguent be? Naturally, there were many who assumed it was butter, but houseboys for the white people thought they recognized it as the cream Madame used on her face and hands. It was very expensive. You could only buy it at the pharmacy. That did wonders for Maboko's prestige.

No one in Kigali was surprised that Maboko had so quickly grown rich, that the proprietor of a little shop in Muhima so soon metamorphosed into a titan of commerce: wasn't he born on the same hill as the president? His rise through the ranks of the Party was just as quick. The unpolished, tangled style of his speeches had come to be considered the authentic voice of the people of the hoe. But the rumors of his wealth were surely exaggerated: to hear people tell it, he owned nearly every taxi in the streets of Kigali, nearly every minibus and pickup on the roads of Rwanda, nearly every semi-truck on the road to Mombasa, there was even talk of a private plane that made mysterious trips back and forth from Kigali to Nairobi. Surely he didn't really win the contract for every single construction project. Still, if you wanted to do business in Rwanda, it was best to first come to an understanding with Maboko Jean de Dieu and Co.

One single detail had nearly put a stop to Maboko's meteoric ascent: his competitors realized he didn't have a first name. The sign on his shop read "Maboko," nothing more. They rightly concluded that he hadn't been baptized, that he was still a pagan. The girls he invited into his shower to scrub his back (and everyone knew how that shower ended) divulged that his bulging stomach was ornamented with scars. It seemed a great scandal that the god of the missionaries should favor a hardened pagan who surely used sorcery to strike deals that would enrich himself at the expense of good Christians. And how could the Party, that cherished child of Christian democracy, count among its members an influential militant who had never been enlightened by the baptismal waters? Sensing the threat, Maboko had himself baptized as quickly and discreetly as he could.

He was given the Christian name Jean de Dieu, and he ordered it to be added to the sign on his store, the sides of his minibuses, the tarps on his trucks. He framed his baptismal certificate and hung it on the wall to the right of the president's portrait. He rented the front row in the cathedral, and had brass plates with his name affixed to the chairs. The god of the Christians – who, as everyone knows, spends all day striding over the globe and then comes home to Rwanda to sleep – could now freely lavish his favors on Maboko Jean de Dieu.

——— ——— ———

And so for a time Helena served as a living sign for the store in Muhima, but soon we stopped seeing her in her glass case. Nor, to the bewilderment of all, was Maboko showing her off in Kigali's chic gathering places: the Bar des Diplomates, the Mille Collines swimming pool. Was Maboko turned afraid of rivals? The word was that Helena had not been unmoved by the distinguished attentions of a young embassy attaché . . . Maboko now preferred to take Helena out to the nightclubs of Bujumbura, on the shores of Lake Tanganyika, and even, since his business often called him to Nairobi, the salons of the Intercontinental. In Kigali, only a few close associates – most particularly those with lucrative deals on the table – had the privilege of coming anywhere near Helena. He used her as a closing argument, for which purpose he installed a salon in the backrooms of his store, a place to receive special guests. The room was furnished with an enormous refrigerator and a long table bearing rows of glasses and bottles of Primus and Johnny Walker; in its center the gilded neck of a magnum of champagne emerged from a huge ice bucket, though it was never uncorked. Red and green leatherette armchairs lined the walls, which were decorated only with the president's portrait. When the guests entered they found Helena standing to the right of the fridge in the diaphanous whiteness of her *invutano*, that elegant ceremonial garb women wear for parties and weddings. She knew how to get the most out of the sheer muslin's translucence, and on her master's instructions she gave an occasional glimpse of her charms, more or less tempting depending on the importance of the business at hand.

But always Helena's main role was to pour drinks – not a menial task in Rwanda, and one that can be performed only by a woman. She had no equal for precisely filling the glasses with beer, whether ice cold, as the white people like it, or warm, as Rwandans prefer. She deftly doled out whisky or Coke depending on the turn the discussion was taking. But above all she took care, obeying the rules of Rwandan politesse, to keep the guest's glass full at all times. She perched herself on a tall barstool, and the moment one of her guests took a sip – that same politesse demanding that you never take more than a sip – she signaled the serving boy manning the refrigerator and drinks table to uncap a fresh bottle, then, bowed low in graceful submission, she poured out exactly as much beer as necessary to top off the glass, tilting it just so to make the requisite crown of foam. Maboko didn't like people speaking to Helena, and her only answer to the jokes of the Rwandans and the banal flirtations of the white people was a smile imprinted with feigned innocence.

Helena's sequestration was the object of more or less universal disapproval in Kigali. Everyone was eagerly waiting for that beautiful creature to run away. They would have liked one of Maboko's competitors – even a white man, why not? – to make off with the poor prisoner, not because they pitied her but simply for the pleasure of seeing fat Maboko cuckolded and belittled. It didn't turn out that way.

——— ——— ———

After the first three years of high school, I was admitted to the college-preparatory class: an exceptional privilege for a Tutsi, which I probably owed to my French teacher. I was his best student. I loved to write, I filled up notebooks with quotations, notes, little stories of my own invention. The teacher read my papers out loud, to the great fury of my classmates, who patiently awaited their chance to avenge themselves. He loaned me a few of his books, books that were banned from the school library, which allowed only uplifting works. Thanks to him, I secretly read Malraux, Sartre, Camus . . .

I took care not to let that get around. But in 1973 came a push to expel all Tutsis from secondary schools, from the university, from the government. The hunt for Tutsis obviously didn't spare Notre-Dame-de-Cîteaux. I found my name at the head of the list of expulsions drawn up by the "Committee for Public Safety," which directed the purge from within the establishment. My Hutu schoolmates brought in a few Party toughs to drive us out of the school with clubs. I took shelter at my French teacher's house. After a time he hid me in the trunk of his car and drove me to the end of a secluded dirt road, not far from the Burundi border. In Bujumbura I was lucky enough to find work as a French teacher at Saint-Albert middle school, funded and run by Rwandan exiles so their children could get an education.

A few months later I heard that Helena too had come to seek refuge in Bujumbura. Taking advantage of the unrest of early 1973, which he had very likely orchestrated, the Minister of Defense and Chief of Staff Juvénal Habyarimana had seized power. Life changes when a new regime comes in. No longer was it a good idea to let it be known that you came from Gitarama, much less to boast that you were born on the same hill as the ex-president. Maboko had a target on his back. They assailed him with big words – corruption, misappropriation, prevarication – whose meaning he didn't fully understand but which led inexorably to the confiscation of his assets. Already a frenzied crowd had seen fit to pillage his store in Muhima. They burned the ex-president's portrait and Maboko's certificate of baptism, which they thought a flagrant forgery. His drivers declared themselves the owners of his vehicles, erasing their fallen boss's name from the doors and replacing it with "Long Live Habyarimana." The Minister of Transport had to move heaven and earth to seize the taxis and trucks for himself. A new crowd of businessmen settled into the salon's green and red armchairs to divide up their competitor's bounty. They finally uncorked the famous magnum and savored a slightly flat champagne. Before they could throw him in prison, Maboko managed to flee to Nairobi, where he emptied the bank accounts he'd opened and filled with cash back in his golden days. The story was that he'd absconded to Belgium. I never heard another word about him.

Helena was very nearly lynched. Youths and hoodlums – along with several respectable matrons, I was told – besieged the little villa Maboko had built for her a few blocks from the store. They threw stones and waved clubs, demanding a public, exemplary punishment for one of those diabolical beauties corrupting the "simple and innocent soul of the people who farmed the thousand hills of Rwanda by the sweat of their brow." Helena had taken the precaution of hiding in a girlfriend's house far from Muhima, in a neighborhood known as Biryago. One morning, a long car with diplomatic plates came and picked her up to take her to Bujumbura. At the border, the policemen respectfully saluted the elegant diplomat who never failed to leave them a little contribution for their Primus. And so they didn't look too closely at the woman wrapped in a filthy *pagne* – a relative of my housegirl, the diplomat had vaguely assured them – sitting in the back seat.

—— —— ——

Bujumbura had lost a good deal of its luster, but it was still the capital of Burundi, and still known as a place where any pleasure could be had. In contrast to austere, pious, cold Kigali, nights on the banks of Lake Tanganyika were warm and lush, with the lamps of the Greek fishermen shimmering on the water. Kigali was then nothing more than a dreary mountain town, whereas Bujumbura prided itself on its cosmopolitan ways. Shaded by the well-tamed luxuriance of their yards, the villas in the posh neighborhoods climbed up the first foothills of the mountains my geography-teacher colleagues called the Congo-Nile chain, for lack of a better name. I never went as far as Kiriri, the rich people's hill: we people from down below were not welcome there, as their dogs, guards, policemen, and soldiers quickly and violently made clear. I could only imagine – from the books I read or the films I went to see at the French or American cultural center – the strange life of that forbidden paradise's inhabitants. Around illuminated pools, diplomats' wives danced in their white-tuxedoed lovers' arms. In smoke-filled salons, Greek shopowners and diamond smugglers won and lost fortunes at poker. In a secluded corner of a garden, beneath a straw-roofed gazebo, young colonels, distant cousins of the sitting president, plotted their next coup d'état . . . And higher still, overlooking all of Kiriri, the Collège du Saint-Esprit, the citadel of the Jesuits, took itself for the gates of heaven.

All around the hill reserved for that privileged few lay the endless neighborhoods of mud and sheet metal: Bwiza, Buyenzi, Mutanga, Kinindo, Kamenge, Nyakabiga, Buhonga, Kanyosha . . . Deep into the night, the harsh light of the pressurized oil lamps called Petromaxes illuminated the little bars, crackling transistor radios pouring out the latest music from Kinshasa or Brazzaville. New to the trade or withered and old, prostitutes flitted around the Primus drinkers like moths drawn to the glow of the oil lamps: *"Agacupa, Bwana, agacupa*: How about a little glass, boss, one little glass!" Out past the Asian district, home to business-obsessed Omanis, Pakistanis, Sikhs, Indians, and Goans, the port and its cranes created a seaside atmosphere immediately belied by the nearness of the mountains on the opposite shore, in what was then called Zaire. Forever blanketed in darkness, said to be the last stronghold of a rebellion that could not be defeated, those mountains seemed to cast a menacing shadow of chaos over the city.

Helena already had a reputation in Bujumbura. Her appearances in the nightclubs had not been forgotten. When she pushed away fat Maboko, too soon out of breath, she would go on dancing alone, and everyone would gather around to admire her, urging her on, clapping their hands. She was the queen of the night. The handsome diplomat came to join her whenever he could. That one knew how to dance! He only went to the nightclub at the Sources du Nil, the just-opened luxury hotel. Impressively proportioned bouncers showed no pity as they filtered the would-be customers. When her lover was away, Helena remained demurely cloistered in the house he'd rented for her, one of those new houses built for government officials, nearby the Bwiza neighborhood and the shops of the city center. Did poor Helena picture herself becoming the lawful wife of the embassy attaché? Was she thinking he would at least carry her away in his bags as his official mistress? Here I would like to write the word "love," like in the French novels I'd read. I don't know what form their separation took when the diplomat was appointed to another post: did he have the courage to say goodbye face to face? Did he merely send her a letter, with a little money enclosed? Or did he just disappear with no forwarding address?

Helena embarked on a career as a high-class call girl. What else could she do? In the teachers' lounge at the Collège Saint-Albert, everyone put on scandalized faces to dissect her latest liaison. She'd been spotted in the bar of the Club Nautique or the Entente Sportive with a banker from the Belgolaise Bank, a Cameroonian FAO official, various French or Belgian volunteers, a pharmacist, a Greek baker, a string of colonels from the Burundian army. To universal disapproval, she was seen for some time in the company of one of those Senegalese or Malian jewelers who are all named N'Gaye and rumored to traffic in human blood. It was almost as if anyone aspiring to any kind of status in the tiny neocolonial society of Bujumbura had to be seen, for a few weeks at least, on Helena's arm. Her former lovers only laughed when some newcomer boasted of his good fortune. Being with Helena was a sort of initiation. When she abandoned him (and it was most often her who initiated the breakup), it was as if he'd been admitted into a very select club.

Like any prostitute, she was an easy target for extortion. Not by the little pimps who stationed their girls on dark streetcorners to whistle at the passing four-by-fours, and not by the patrols of the Rwagasore Revolutionary Youth, who exacted a tribute from what they called "free women" in the name of public morality. No, Helena's persecutor was the Sûreté, the national police. She was often discreetly summoned to headquarters, no doubt to demand a tax payment in cash or in kind, but above all to hear her report on her lovers. Threatened with prison or expulsion (refugee status was always a precarious thing), there was no way she could refuse those omnipotent policemen who made all of Bujumbura tremble, and to whom, without proof, more than one unexplained disappearance was attributed. That became particularly clear to us when Mobutu Sese Seko came for a state visit.

The Burundian authorities looked with deep trepidation on the visits of the President of Zaire, Mobutu Sese Seko Kuku Ngbendu Wa Za Banga. They didn't want to be drawn into the turmoils of their giant neighbor to the west, and they tried to find ways to ward off the unpredictable demands the Leopard of Kinshasa would surely make of them. So they were determined to give that redoubtable chief of state a reception as grandiose as the government's finances would allow, and possibly more. Everyone knew he wouldn't be dazzled – though he wasn't yet marshal, he'd seen his share of official welcomes – but they hoped that with plenty of elaborately staged ceremonies, rapturous crowds, interminable speeches and banquets, there wouldn't be much time left over to raise troublesome subjects. All of Bujumbura was mobilized to prepare for the visit. The avenues were decked with banana leaves and bougainvillea flowers, triumphal arches were erected, banners were hung to welcome the illustrious guest. Men were given shirts, and women *pagnes*, ornamented with the two presidents' faces. The chief of protocol urged all government officials to abandon the suit and tie in favor of the *abacost*, Mobutu's trademark garb, an expression of Zairean authenticity. The orchestras and choirs that filled the airwaves with songs of praise for the leader of Burundi now hurried to come up with panegyrics for President Mobutu. Drums – the purest symbol of power – were beaten all day long in the stadium, the drummers dressed in the Party colors of red and white and trying to outdo each other with their acrobatics. Guided by North Korean specialists in mass choreography, the grade school children created living pictures for the glory of the two heads of state. We already knew to applaud after his speech's every sentence. A chartered plane had brought in the food for the banquet, along with cases of champagne and fine wine. All that was left was to decide who would be offered up for the Night of the Minotaur.

A committee was convened to make that very sensitive decision: the chief of protocol, a few ministers' wives, the agents of the Sûreté. And also Floriane, whom I knew because I often ran into her at the library of the French cultural center. Floriane enjoyed a great prestige among the society women of Bujumbura, not because she was distantly related to the royal family, which was no advantage under the First Republic, but because she'd once modeled in Paris under the name Rebecca Darling. People sought her out for advice on hair styles, makeup, what to wear and what not. And so Floriane's job would be to ready the woman chosen to share the Leopard of Kinshasa's bed.

It wasn't a difficult choice. Obviously, she couldn't be from Burundi (although it was said there was no lack of applicants). The national honor would never allow it, not even for the sake of the country's survival. What Burundian mother would ever abandon her daughter to that fate? And then later on, who would dare to marry the poor child and brave the ridicule it would bring? But neither could she be from Zaire, even if many of that country's women dreamed of bedding their beloved leader. In Bujumbura, Mobutu might take serious offense at that: a Zairoise offered up by the people of Burundi! So the women of Zaire are no better than prostitutes!

There was only one choice, then: she had to be a Rwandan. Everyone agreed that the Rwandan refugees owed them that, they couldn't say no: "We took them in, we gave them shelter, their children get an education in our schools, their merchants grow rich at our expense, and they couldn't even manage to defend themselves." Silent until now, the agents of the Sûreté spoke up: "We've got just what you need," they announced. "Helena."

Relieved, the committee unanimously voted their approval.

So Helena was brought as discreetly as possible to the offices of the Sûreté. They explained what they wanted from her. At first she tried to refuse. They promised her many things if she consented, and threatened her with many more if she didn't. They observed that the streets of Bwiza weren't always safe, you could run into some rough characters there. Helena had no choice but to give in. The officers had her rehearse the words she would repeat into the presidential ear. They particularly dwelled on what not to say. "The Sûreté has big ears," they concluded. "We'll know everything you say and everything you don't."

Helena was taken to the military hospital. All the doctors and male nurses volunteered to examine her. The job went to the surgeon-major: "State secret," he decreed. It must have been a very thorough examination; certainly it seemed to take forever to the little uniformed crowd waiting outside his office. Finally the door opened: "Fit for service!" cried the surgeon-major, who had studied in France.

For the choice of Helena's garb, the chief of protocol consulted the women who were considered the most elegant in Bujumbura. They fell into two camps. One urged authenticity, in accordance with the return to tradition that Mobutu Sese Seko had vigorously imposed on the Congo-turned-Zaire; the other, what we might call the Western camp, was headed by Floriane, who drew her inspiration from the top models she'd seen in *Elle* or *Amina*. The first camp wanted her hair plaited into magnificent arabesques and her body clad in a wax print sent straight from the Matongé neighborhood of Brussels. She wouldn't even need panties, they said, since our foremothers never wore them. The other camp pushed for straightened hair, a miniskirt, and a garter belt like in the films the monsignor forbade. Their endless discussions finally arrived at a compromise: Helena would wear a *pagne*, but her hair would be straightened, and she would wear panties. The Burundians weren't about to relinquish what civilization had brought them.

The Hôtel Sources du Nil was requisitioned for Mobutu and his entourage. The president would occupy the entire top floor. A chief of the Sûreté delivered Helena to Mobutu's bodyguards, who undressed her and searched her and brought her to Mobutu's aide-de-camp. He carefully studied Helena from every conceivable angle; when he turned away he seemed visibly disappointed. "This is the best the Burundians could do?" he sighed. "Oh well, we'll see . . . go on and get dressed." They closed Helena up in a linen closet, among the spare sheets, blankets, and pillows. "If you want a Coke or you have to pee," said the sentinel assigned to her, "don't call out, just knock on the door."

Helena sat down on a pile of pillows in the dark, waiting. Finally the hallway outside burst to life. She heard slamming doors, voices, orders in Lingala or French. Then calm returned, and all was quiet again. She heard footsteps approaching the closet. The door opened: "All right, come on," said the aide-de-camp, "he's waiting . . ."

Helena found herself in a dim salon. A floor lamp switched on, and under its broad gilded-silk shade she saw a man in a brightly colored dressing gown sitting in a high-backed armchair. She recognized Mobutu by his leopard-skin toque. An ivory-knobbed cane leaned against one arm of the chair.

"You speak Lingala?"

"No, your Excellency."

"I see. I suppose you're a Rwandan, a Tutsi, like we see too many of in Kinshasa. Take off your *pagne*."

Helena let her *pagne* slip to the floor.

"Come closer," said Mobutu, "and take off your panties."

The ivory knob ran over Helena's body.

"Turn around."

The ivory knob skimmed Helena's back and hips.

Mobutu rapped the floor with his cane. The aide-de-camp came running.

"Too skinny," said Mobutu. "No bottom. Burundians have no idea what a beautiful woman is. Get her out of here!"

Helena put on her *pagne* and followed the aide-de-camp out the door, trembling. At the end of the hallway, he turned around to her:

"Come with me," he said. "I never mind taking the president's leftovers."

Other versions were told of that Night of the Minotaur, as I liked to call the night Helena was offered up to Mobutu. Mine might have been a little too strongly influenced by my readings. I never showed anyone the notebook I wrote it down in. Most of the Rwandan exile community was disgusted: Helena had brought shame to us all. Her wanton life had led her to the most sordid depths: she'd prostituted herself – even if, as some conceded, she did so under duress – for the benefit of the Burundians! But there were some who took her defense: Bible-toting Protestants compared her to Queen Esther, the favorite wife of Ahasuerus, King of Persia, she who had saved the Jewish people from extermination. The elders recalled that tradition said our kings had always let their blood be spilled on enemy soil to protect Rwanda from invasion: those were the savior kings, the Abatabazi. No doubt the analogies were questionable, but at least they salvaged Helena's honor.

——— ——— ———

Many in Bujumbura rejoiced in Helena's downfall, the women particularly. Outlandish rumors on the subject of that night with Mobutu scared off the white men, who once considered having Helena as a mistress a source of prestige. No one wanted to be seen with a state prostitute. It might not be safe. Some said she was an informer for the Sûreté. "Stay away from that girl, whatever you do," newcomers were advised. "She'll stick her nose into your business, she might try to blackmail you, in any case she's trouble." The doormen turned her away from the nightclub at the Sources du Nil. She was told in no uncertain terms that that the bars of the Club Nautique and the Entente Sportive had to watch their reputation, and she was no longer welcome there. All that was left was the Pagidas, an old grand hotel from the colonial days that proudly displayed the date of its opening: 1929. Trysts were set up in the men's bathroom, but to get to the customers' rooms you had to pay off the bands of hoodlums who shared the little houses hidden beneath the flamboyants and avocado trees. Helena proudly refused to submit. They threatened to cut up her face: "You see this knife?" said a little man with a limp who seemed to be the leader. "If you ever come back here your good looks are history." And to show her he wasn't joking, he gave her a long slash on her right cheek.

And so Helena lost most of what she'd got out of life. She was forced to give up her beautiful house at the edge of the Bwiza district, on a paved, lit street, a house that could legitimately claim to belong to the "evolved" part of the city. Now she and four newcomers to the trade shared a shabby mud hut deep in the heart of Bwiza, at the end of a little street whose ruts were so deep no car would ever drive down it. Helena soon became a focus of curious interest in the neighborhood. Office workers, shopkeepers, taxi drivers, houseboys, and footsoldiers all wanted to sleep with the woman who'd once been a favorite of the white people but who supposedly Mobutu wanted no part of. That was a great subject of conversation in the local bars: who was right, the white people or Mobutu? University students took up collections so that once a week one of them could, as they said, "write his paper" on the Great Whore. Finally Helena fled Bwiza and found refuge with an old Italian garage owner who worked on taxis and dilapidated trucks.

——— ——— ———

I was just finishing my grading when I noticed a little girl sitting on my front step. Clearly, she hadn't dared interrupt me. I asked what she wanted.

"I have a note for you," she answered. "It's from Helena."

She held out the sheet, folded in four. I had some difficulty making out the few words: "Do you remember Kirarambogo? You must come and see me at the Italo Garage, in the Asian district. I'm expecting you."

"Tell Helena I'll be there tomorrow."

I scoured the Asian district's busy streets in vain, looking for the Italo Garage. Finally someone told me it must be in the vacant lots between the port and the last houses of the neighborhood. The garage turned out to be a huge yard ringed by high walls studded with broken glass. Two big, barking dogs raced toward me, throwing themselves against the sheet-metal and grillwork gate at the entrance. A white-haired man in oil-stained coveralls came running:

"What do you want?"

"I've come to see Helena."

"Oh, all right, I'll go see."

I waited for a long time. The dogs threatened me with their foam-flecked fangs, their front legs hooked over the gate's grillwork. Finally the aged mechanic came back, tied up the dogs, and cracked open the gate.

"The boss says you can come in."

A pyramid of rusting, stripped-down cars took up half of the yard. Under a roofed work area, a white man, also dressed in grimy coveralls, pulled his head from under the hood of an old VW Bug and stared at me in silence, studying me, I thought, from head to toe.

"You recognize me, Asumpta? You haven't forgotten me?"

"How could I have forgotten you?"

"Kirarambogo's such a long way away."

"Yes, a long way."

"What do you think of me today?"

I gave her a long look. Yes, she was still as beautiful as ever, but I couldn't help noticing how terribly thin she'd become. Her face still had its golden glow, maybe thanks to makeup, but I could see the grayish tint of her hands and arms.

"Beautiful as ever."

"Don't tell me how beautiful I am. It was beauty that brought me here, here to this prison, which will also be my last refuge. Old Italo couldn't believe it when he saw me show up. He'd bought so many martinis for the girls at Les Coconuts, and it never got him anywhere. He couldn't understand why someone like me would want to move in with the lowliest white man in town. But I couldn't stay in Bwiza with all those men – even the little marketplace thieves – wanting to sleep with me just to humiliate me. And whenever I went out, the children followed me in the street, whistling and singing:

> *There goes the Great Whore,*
> *She's Mobutu's whore.*
> *But old Sek Seko,*
> *'Too skinny,' said he,*
> *'Too skinny,' said he.*

"So this is a place where no one will ever come, there are walls, there are dogs, Italo says he has a rifle he killed elephants with when he was young. He gives me food, he goes to the market and buys me secondhand clothes and tubes of Venus de Milo. Don't tell me how beautiful I am. I've broken my mirror. I wish I could have broken my face along with it."

"Don't say that, Helena, you're hurting yourself."

"Listen, Asumpta, I didn't ask you here just to tell you my troubles. We're Tutsis, sorrow hangs over all of us, and it lands heaviest of all on the women. There's nothing we can do. Maybe things will be different one day. I won't see that day. But I hope Kadogo will."

"Kadogo?"

"My son. He's half-white. His father was gone by the time he was born. I didn't tell him. He was an important white man. A big official at the embassy. He wouldn't have wanted anything to do with my Kadogo. You understand, with the life I was leading, the boy couldn't stay with me. I left him with an old mama from back home, or almost, from Makwaza. Now he's big, and I want him to go to school. I pay for his room and board, and when the time comes I'll pay for his tuition and anything else he might need. But suppose I'm not around – and I believe death has already given me the nod – then who will take care of my Kadogo? I don't want him becoming one of those boys who beg at the post-office door, one of those boys who wash windshields, and besides he's half-white . . . So promise me, when I'm gone, will you look after Kadogo? One day soon you'll be married, you'll have children, could you find room in your family for Kadogo?"

"Yes, Helena, I promise, Kadogo will be my first son, but believe me, you'll see him grow up. He needs you."

―― ―― ――

In Bujumbura, the fashion was for funeral processions to make a great show of creeping at a snail's pace through the streets. Cars and pedestrians were supposed to stop in their tracks. I'm talking of course about the funerals of what I call the rich and powerful. Behind the truck that carried the coffin, you could see fancy Range

Rovers and Mercedes, army jeeps, taxis, minibuses, Toyota pickups . . . Even more than wedding parades, funeral processions were a chance to show off the family's influence, their noble lineage, their vast clan. But today those displays have become more discreet. There are too many deaths. Too many deaths for people to go on blaming poisoners or West Africans and the strange sicknesses they always bring. AIDS, the white people call it, supposedly it came from monkeys, but we can't quite believe that the Pygmies ever made love with gorillas. Here we call AIDS Agakoko, a little invisible animal that gets inside you, like termites, and once it's in you it gnaws away at you, it gnaws, gnaws, gnaws . . . The catechists and the Bible-readers tell us it's a punishment sent from God. Just look at the first ones who caught it, they say: "second offices," "free women," and the street-walkers who whistle under the mango trees. Then they passed it on to their customers, adulterers, libertines: they became tools for the wrath of God.

The mayor of Bujumbura has taken things in hand. He's made it his mission to restore morality to the streets of the city: day and night, the Rwagasore Revolutionary Youth, backed by commando squads of out-of-work young people hired and armed with clubs by the mayor, go miniskirt hunting. That indecent fashion must have been the drop of water that made the vase of God's wrath overflow. The mayor's young people delight in that new sport. Whenever they get their hands on a girl in a miniskirt they pull it up over her hips, rip away the little piece of fabric beneath it, and give her an enthusiastic beating with their sticks. Most often that happens in the marketplace. The women buying and selling meekly look away; the children who offer their services carrying baskets in exchange for a few coins pelt the poor girl with rotten tomatoes and papayas as she silently chokes back her sorrow and shame. After dark, the raids on nightclubs are aimed mostly at homosexuals: if they're black they go to prison, if they're white they're handed their expulsion papers the next day.

I bring up AIDS because I'm convinced it had a hand in Helena's death. Helena didn't die of AIDS, even if she was probably sick with it, but AIDS was the cause of her murder. According to the newspaper – there's only one in Burundi – it was the Gatalinas, the notorious gang of thieves, that attacked Italo's garage. Everyone knows about those bandits, who spread terror all through Bujumbura: they use a big rock to break down the doors of the houses they want to pillage. "Gatalina! Gatalina!" they shout. Gatalina – Catherine – is evidently what they call the big rock they use as a battering ram, just as the hurricanes that ravage America always have women's names. The paper said the police found the garage's gate beaten down, the two dogs shot with a revolver. The old mechanic who served as a night watchman was nowhere to be seen. Italo had been tied to a chair, blindfolded and gagged. He swore he'd seen nothing, heard nothing. They'd beaten him over the head. He couldn't remember anything. They found Helena's body in the grease pit. She was naked. The doctor said she'd been stabbed more than ten times in the belly and breasts.

Few of us believed the official version we read in the paper. No one could understand why the Gatalinas should attack a pauper like Italo, why they should go after Helena so viciously. And what about the revolver? The Gatalinas had machetes, but certainly not revolvers, especially not the kind policemen carry in their holsters.

So there's another theory, of course. People only speak of it in hushed tones, when they're sure no one's listening. Whoever attacked the garage, they weren't there to rob Italo, they were there to take their revenge on Helena. They thought it was Helena who had given them AIDS, Helena who had caused the death of their brother, their friend . . . Killing Helena was like eradicating AIDS. We've all heard those boasts in the bars. Drunken students and their army friends, celebrating the execution of the Great Whore.

——— ——— ———

I look across the table at Kadogo doing his homework, and I know he'll soon be asking once again, "Asumpta, what was my mama like?" and I'll tell him, "Your mama, Kadogo, she was beautiful, very beautiful."

Grief

On the TV, on the radio, they never called it genocide. As if that word were reserved. Too serious. Too serious for Africa. Yes, there were massacres, but there were always massacres in Africa. And these massacres were happening in a country no one had ever heard of. A country no one could find on a map. Tribal hatreds, primitive, atavistic hatreds: nothing to understand there. "Some weird stuff is going on where you come from," people would tell her.

She herself didn't know the word, but in Kinyarwanda there was a very old term for what was happening in her homeland: *gutsem-batsemba*, a verb, used for talking about parasites and mad dogs, things that had to be eradicated, and about Tutsis, also known as Inyenzi, cockroaches, also something to be wiped out. She remembered the story her Hutu schoolmates had told her, laughing, at high school in Kigali: "Someday a child will ask his mother, 'Tell me, Mama, who were those Tutsis I keep hearing about? What did they look like?' and the mother will answer, 'They weren't anything at all, my son, those are just stories.'"

Nevertheless, she hadn't lost hope. She wanted to know. Her father, her mother, her brothers, her sisters, her whole family back in Rwanda – some of them might still be alive, maybe for now the slaughter had spared them, maybe they'd managed to escape into exile, as she had? Her parents on the hill had no telephone, of course, but she called one of her brothers who taught in Ruhengeri. The phone rang and rang. No one answered. She called her sister in Butare, who'd married a shopkeeper. A voice she'd never heard before told her, "There's nobody here." She called her brother in Canada. He was the oldest. If their parents were dead, then he'd be the head of the family. Maybe he had news, maybe he had advice, maybe he could help her begin to face her terror. They spoke, and then they fell silent. What was there to say? From now on, they were alone.

From now on, she would be alone. She knew a few people from home, of course, friends she'd made at the university where she'd started her studies all over again, her African degrees being worthless in France. But there was a little part of her – the part that still tied her to those she'd left behind in Rwanda – that despite the distance and the time gone by and the impossibility of rejoining them made a bond that grounded her identity and affirmed her in her will to go on. Those bonds would fade, and in the cold of her solitude their disappearance would leave her somehow amputated.

She felt very fragile. "I'm like an egg," she often told herself. "One jolt and I'll break." She moved as sparingly as she could, she lived in slow motion. She walked as if she were seeking her way in the dark, as if at any moment she might run into an obstacle and fall to the ground. Climbing a staircase took a tremendous effort: a great weight lay on her shoulders. She found herself counting the steps she still had to climb, clutching the banister as if she were at the edge of an abyss, and when she reached her floor she was breathless and drained.

She tried to find an escape in mindless household tasks. Again and again, she maniacally straightened her studio apartment. Something was always where it shouldn't be: books on the couch, shoes in the entryway, Rwandan nesting baskets untidily lined up on the shelf. She was sure she'd feel better if everything was finally where it belonged. But she was forever having to go back and start over again.

If only she had at least a picture of her parents. She rifled through the little suitcase that had come with her through all her travels. There were letters, there were notebooks filled with words, useless diplomas, even her Rwandan identity card, with the "Tutsi" stamp that she'd tried to scratch away. There were a handful of photographs of her with her girlfriends in Burundi (they'd had them taken at a photographer's in the Asian district in Bujumbura, before they parted ways, so they wouldn't forget), there were postcards sent by her brother in Canada, a few pages of a diary she'd soon abandoned, but she never did find a photo of her parents.

For that she rebuked herself bitterly. Why hadn't she thought to ask them to have their picture taken and send her a copy? Was she a neglectful daughter? Had she forgotten them as the years went by? No, they were still there in her memory, she could call up their image anytime she liked. She sat down at her table, took her head in her hands, closed her eyes, focused her mind, and pictured, one by one, all the faces that death might already have erased.

——— ——— ———

Then, toward the end of June, she got a letter. There was no mistaking where it came from: the red-and-blue bordered envelope, the exotic bird on the stamp, the clumsily written address . . . She couldn't bring herself to open it. She put it on her bookshelf, behind the Rwandan baskets. She pretended to forget it. There were so many more urgent and more important things to do: make dinner, iron a pair of jeans, organize her class notes. But the letter was still there, behind the baskets. Suddenly she found herself tearing open the envelope. She pulled out a sheet of square-ruled paper, a page from a schoolchild's notebook. She didn't need to read the few sentences that served as an introduction to a long list of names: her father, her mother, her brothers, her sisters, her uncles, her aunts, her nephews, her nieces . . . Henceforth that would be the list of her dead, of everyone who had died far away from her, without her, and there was nothing she could do for them, not even die with them. She stared at the letter, unable to weep, and she began to think it was sent by the dead themselves. It was a message from the land of the dead. And this, she thought, would probably be their only grave, a column of names she didn't even need to reread because those names she knew so well echoed in her head like cries of pain.

She kept the letter from her dead with her at all times. She never showed it to anyone. Whenever someone asked, "What happened to your family?" she always answered, "They were killed, they're all dead, every one." And when they asked how she'd heard, she told them, "I just know, that's all, don't ask me anything more." She often felt the need to touch that piece of paper. She stared at the column of names, not reading them, with no tears in her eyes, and the names filled her head with pleas that she didn't know how to answer.

What she didn't want to see: pictures on television, photos in newspapers and magazines, corpses lying by roadsides, dismembered bodies, faces slashed by machetes. What she didn't want to hear: any rumor that might summon up images of the frenzy of sex and blood that had crashed over the women, the girls, the children . . .

She wanted to protect her dead, to keep them untouched in her memory, their bodies whole and unsullied, like the saints she'd heard about at catechism, miraculously preserved from corruption.

Most of all she didn't want to sleep, because to fall asleep was to deliver herself to the killers. Every night they were there. They'd taken over her sleep, they were the masters of her dreams. They had no faces; they came toward her in a gray, blood-soaked throng. Or else they had just one single face, an enormous face that laughed viciously as it pressed to hers, crushing her.

No, no going to sleep.

Of course, she should have wept. She owed the dead that. If she wept, she could be close by their side. She imagined them waiting behind the veil of tears, nearby and unreachable. Maybe that was why she'd gone so far away from them, why she'd headed off into exile: there had to be someone to weep for all those whose memory the killers had tried to erase, whose existence they'd tried to deny. But she couldn't weep.

"You know what," one of her friends told her, "my father just died."

"I'll go to his funeral," she answered, without thinking.

She was immediately sorry she'd made that promise. Was it right for her to honor someone else's dead if she couldn't weep for her own? In her mind she summoned up images of Rwandan women weeping over their lost loved ones, able to weep because the body was there before them, before it was put in the ground. Yes, the women of Rwanda knew how to mourn. First they wept sitting up very straight, still and silent, their tears falling like raindrops from eucalyptus trees. Then came the keening and wailing; the women shivered and quaked, racked head to toe by violent sobs. Finally they huddled beneath their *pagnes*, disappearing, silent but for their sighs as they choked back their tears, and then even that waned little by little. Now the loved one could enter the land of the dead. He'd got the tears he was deserved, and although the pain of the loss was still there, you knew it would begin to grow more discreet, you'd be able to live with it, and the lost loved one would leave a more peaceful memory in the world of the living, a welcoming memory, maybe that's what the white people meant when they talked about the grieving process.

With that he was allowed to set off for his final home. The body was carried on an *ingobyi*, a long stretcher made of bamboo slats. The women would keep their eyes fixed on the lost one, accompanying him on his voyage as if they had to lend him their aid one last time before he he was welcomed into the other world, the unknown world of the spirits. The *ingobyi* also served as a bride's palanquin on her wedding day. She too was expected to weep. As she was taken from her parents' house to her new family, her sobs – too loud to be sincere – showed everyone that she was leaving the paternal enclosure against her wishes. The *ingobyi* always demanded its tribute of tears.

She sadly remembered the little cemetery where she and her companions in exile once liked to meet. This was in Bujumbura, at the little seminary where they'd temporarily been taken in. In exchange for a half-hearted hospitality, the four refugee girls did housekeeping, helped in the kitchen, served the abbots at dinner, washed dishes. They tried to ward off the insistent curiosity of the seminarians, made restless by the presence of girls. They were forever having to invent new excuses to turn down the abbots' invitations to come pick out a book or have a little talk in their rooms. When the siesta hour came they went out into the garden to talk about all that had happened to them and to consider their uncertain future. Beyond the banana grove they discovered a little forgotten cemetery with a handful of wooden crosses. The white paint was peeling, and the black letters of the names had almost entirely faded. "Let's say a prayer," said Espérance. "You always have to do something for the dead."

They came back to those graves day after day. The little cemetery became their secret domain, their refuge, a safe place, far from the irritable stares of the miserly old nun, far from the indiscreet, ardent gazes of the abbots and seminarians. They pulled the weeds from the graves, they laid purple flowers cut from the bougainvillea that climbed up the façade of the father superior's little house. "These could be our parents' graves," said Eugénie. "They might have been killed. Maybe because of us, because we went away, they might have been killed." They stood side by side, they held each other in the style of a Rwandan greeting. Then they all burst into tears, and that shared lament brought them some comfort and solace.

They would hurry out to the little cemetery early in the afternoon, as soon as the dishes were washed and the siesta hour had begun. They'd each chosen a grave of their own. Sometimes it was their parents', sometimes a brother's, a sister's, a fiancé's . . . And they mourned their absence, or possibly their death, if it turned out they'd been killed in reprisal for the girls' going away. The dirt was cracked and eroded from the heat and the rain, so they covered the graves with pebbles taken a handful at a time from the wide walkway that led to the calvary. They found a few slightly chipped vases in the sacristy, and they placed them before the graves' crosses, which they'd carefully straightened. They filled the vases with flowers they'd borrowed from the altar of the Holy Virgin. And then, sitting before the graves, their arms around their legs, their chins on their knees, they silently let their tears flow, always a little afraid that a seminarian might happen on to them and mock them for their strange rituals.

Long after that little group of refugees was scattered into different schools she still missed the haven she'd found in that little cemetery. And today, she realized how much she wished she could be back by those strangers' graves, where she'd shed so many tears.

———— ———— ————

There was a sort of minivan, of a discreet, elegant gray, parked before the porch of the church. Two men in dark suits were waiting, bored, on the steps. She went inside and tiptoed down the side aisle until she reached an empty chair with a view of the choir and the altar. She saw a priest standing at a microphone, talking about the consolation of an afterlife. Nothing to do with her dead. She spotted her friend in the front row, no doubt surrounded by her family. She was shocked to see that the women weren't weeping, although some had red eyes, and she was sorry to find that they weren't draped in the elaborate mourning veils she'd seen in old photos. The men were all wearing grave expressions that seemed forced to her.

Soon her eye was drawn to the coffin, which was sitting on a little pedestal, armfuls of flowers laid out all around it. She couldn't help admiring the coffin's gleaming, polished wood, its elegant molding, its gilded handles. The old man must have been lying in that padded box dressed in his best suit, and maybe, as she'd heard tell, maybe they'd made up his face so they could tell themselves death was only a restful sleep. She began to hate that old man, who'd died a painless death, her friend had told her – "a good death," as she said over and over. And as she stared at the coffin she felt as if she could see inside it, as if the wood had turned transparent. And the body she saw in that silken, gently lit bubble was her father's body, dressed in the spotless *pagne* that marked him as an elder and the white shirt he wore for Sunday mass. Suddenly she felt tears rolling down her cheeks, and she heard a loud sob escape her. Now there was no stopping it. She let the tears flow, she didn't try to hold them back or wipe them away. It was as if a wave of solace had erupted from the very heart of her sorrow. She couldn't stop whispering the lamentation that accompanies the dead in Rwanda. She could feel her neighbors' uncomfortable, reproachful stares. She heard a murmur run through the rows before her and behind her. She fled, now and then jostling a kneeling woman as she hurried past. Her footfalls resounded against the stone floor as if to denounce her: what right did she have to weep for that man she didn't know, that man surrounded by a family who mourned him with a proper, polite sadness? She was a parasite of their grief.

She wished she could forget what had happened at the church: that vision of her father's corpse, her fit of tears. She avoided her friend so she wouldn't have to answer her questions. But a strange thought filled her head, insistent, obsessive, convincing her that her dead had given her a sign, and she was afraid to understand too clearly what they were trying to tell her. Nonetheless, she found that the long strolls she liked to take through the streets of the city inevitably brought her to a church, where she always hoped to see a gleaming gray or black hearse parked in front. And more than once she did, and then an irresistible force drew her inside, with the crowd of mourners. She knew just where to sit: always behind a pillar, but always with a view of the coffin. She stared at it long and hard, hoping she might once again see through the wood and find one of her dead inside it: her mother wrapped in her *pagne*, her little sister in her schoolgirl dress . . . It didn't always work, but the tears came every time. And she was convinced that because she was there with them, those who had come to mourn a son killed in a traffic accident or a brother dead after what they called a long illness or a father felled by a heart attack would also weep for her dead, just a little. *And in exchange*, she told herself, *I'm joining in their sorrow for the one they lost. They can't possibly mind.*

She thought her dead wanted her to be present at funerals so they too could have their share of mourning and tears. Once she never read the newspaper; now she opened it feverishly every morning to read the obituaries. She became a regular at the church near her apartment. That went on for some months, but eventually her strangely faithful attendance was noticed. One day, as she was trying to discreetly leave the church, a young priest stopped her outside the front door:

"Madame, if you please . . ."

She couldn't push him away, and she couldn't go back inside.

"Madame, if you please, allow me, I'd like a word with you . . . I've noticed that you come to almost every funeral, and that you weep as if you knew the deceased. That can be upsetting for the families, for everyone who's suffered a loss. Perhaps I can help you? I'd like nothing more than to listen to you, help you . . . if there's anything I can do . . ."

"No, leave me alone, I promise you'll never see me again."

She wandered the city streets, now become the labyrinth of her despair, with no way out. She thought that the very tenuous, very frail bonds that connected her to her own dead through the losses of others were now broken forever. She felt herself sinking into an aloneness that would never end. All she had left was that piece of notebook paper, now badly crumpled, and that list of names she couldn't bring herself to read but endlessly whispered to herself like a hypnotic refrain of sadness and remorse.

She went home and tried to immerse herself in her most recent class notes, to neatly copy them out on a fresh sheet of paper, but she found the names of her dead filling the page. Now she was afraid:

she was going to lose her mind, she already had lost her mind, these things she'd been doing weren't what her dead wanted at all. They weren't here, in this land of exile, in these foreign churches, they were waiting back home, in the land of the dead that Rwanda had become. They were waiting for her. She would go to them.

——— ——— ———

"Stop," she told the driver, "this is the place. That's the path to my house, and if you keep going it takes you up to the eucalyptus plantings at the very top of the hill. And that hut over there at the side of the road, that's Népomucène's cabaret, he sold banana beer and Fanta, even Primus sometimes, but not often. One time, I remember it to this day, my father bought me an orange Fanta when he came back from the market, he must have got a good price for his coffee."

"You really want to go there?" the driver sighed. "You know, it's no use, there's nothing left, it might not be good for you. In any case, you shouldn't go by yourself: you never know, you might run into a madman, and besides there are people who still want to 'finish the job,' so being there all alone, with those people who died up there . . ."

"I made a promise. Maybe I'll find what I've come here for . . . I promised, I have to go."

"I'll come back this evening, before the sun goes down. I'll honk, and then I'll wait for ten minutes, look, I have a watch just like you do, ten minutes, no more. I've got people waiting for me too, at home."

"I'll be there. See you this evening."

The Toyota pickup drove off in a cloud of red dust, loaded with bananas, mattresses, sheet metal, maybe ten passengers, with a few goats squeezed in. Little by little, the noise of the engine faded away. She spent a long moment looking around her. The dirt road snaked along between the hillside and the swamp, but the shallows where her mother once grew sweet potatoes and corn were now clogged with reeds and papyrus. Népomucène's cabaret was a ruin, its flaking mud walls showing their skeleton of interlaced bamboo. The start of the path up the hill was half-hidden by tall fronds of dried grass. For a moment she wondered if this really was Gihanga. But soon she got hold of herself. She should have known that everything would be different: death had come to this place, it was death's domain now.

The hill was steep, but the path soon turned rocky, and the tangle of brush that first slowed her down gradually thinned. She tried to make out what were once cultivated parcels of land in the thick growth that had invaded the hillside. The plots marked off for the coffee plants were easy to spot, but shaggy, disheveled bushes bore witness to their abandonment. A few oversized, sterile maniocs still rose up from the weeds smothering the last stalks of sorghum.

Halfway up the hill, in the middle of abandoned fields, a patch of almost impenetrable forest still survived. Fig trees towered over the sea of pointed dracaena leaves. Her father had told her those were the vestiges of an old king's enclosure. This place was now haunted by his *umuzimu*, his spirit, and he might have been reincarnated in the python that guarded this sacred woods where no one dared set foot. "Stay away," said the old ones. "The python has been furious ever since the *abapadris* forbade us to bring it offerings. If you go near him, he'll swallow you!" She couldn't help thinking that this gloomy forest and its python were now the masters of the hill, and they would end up devouring her.

She reached the stand of banana trees, whose glossy leaves once concealed the enclosure. Many of the trees had fallen, dull brown with rot. The leaves of those still standing hung tattered and yellow. A few of them still bore sad, stunted fruit.

She found her pace slowing as she neared the enclosure. She wasn't sure she'd have the strength to see this journey through to the end, to face firsthand what she'd already been told of. But now she was standing by the palisade. The wall of interlaced branches had collapsed and come apart, but what were once uprights were now shrubs with vigorous greenery or scarlet flowers, which struck her as indecent, as if, she thought, those simple stakes had come to life on the death of the people who had planted them. Nothing was left of the rectangular main house but a shattered stretch of wall. She searched for some trace of the hearth and its three stones, but she found only a little pile of broken tiles. She couldn't hold back a surge of pride: somehow her father had roofed his house with tiles! But she also observed that the killers had gone to the trouble of taking most of them away. They had all kinds of reasons for murdering their neighbors: they were Tutsis, they had a house with a tile roof. In the back courtyard, the three big grain baskets were slashed and overturned, and the calves' stable was a mound of ash and charred straw. Not wanting to break them any further, she took care not to walk on the shards littering the ground, all that remained of the big jugs the family once used to collect rainwater. Among the debris of the collapsed awning that once covered the hearth, she thought she saw a patch of fabric and hoped it might be a piece of her mother's *pagne*. But when she came closer she realized it was only a yellowed taro leaf.

She knew she wouldn't find what she was looking for in the ruined enclosure. As soon as she'd got to the main town, before making for the hamlet of Gihanga, she'd headed straight for the mission church where the Tutsis had sought shelter, where they'd been slaughtered. Four thousand, five thousand, no one quite knew. Outside the front door she'd seen a little old man with a white beard and a broad, fringed straw hat sitting behind a wooden table. He was the guardian of the dead. He had a notebook in front of him. Visitors were invited to write a few words on their way out, like at an art gallery. The old man gave her a long stare, nodded, then finally said:

"I know you, you're Mihigo's daughter. Did you come to see the dead?"

"Yes, they were calling me."

"You won't find them here. Here there's only death."

"Let me go in."

"Of course, who could deny you that? I'll come with you, follow me, but then I have something to tell you."

"As you see," said the old man, "the *abapadris* and their houseboys washed everything clean, there's nothing left, not one drop of blood, not on the walls, not on the altar. There might still be some in the folds of the Virgin Mary's veil, if you look closely. Once it was all cleaned up, the monsignor came. He wanted mass to be said here again, like before. All it would take was a little holy water. But the survivors objected. They said: 'Where was your God when they were killing us? The white soldiers came to take the priests away, and he went off with them. He won't be back. Now the church belongs to our dead.' The mayor and the prefect agreed. It seems they're going to turn it into a house just for our dead – a memorial, they called it. I'll show you where our dead are waiting in the meantime."

He took a key hung over his neck by a string and opened a door behind the altar, at the back of the apse. Behind it was a vast, dark room stacked to the ceiling with big bags, like for carrying charcoal.

"These are for skulls," said the guide, pointing at the bags against the wall to his left, "and the ones straight ahead of you are for bones. We've got everyone who was here in the church, and all the bones we could find in the hills, left behind by the jackals and abandoned dogs. Even the schoolchildren went off to gather bones during vacations and days off. I hear there are going to be display cases, like at the Pakistani's shop on the marketplace. Your family's here in these bags, but no one can tell you whose bones are whose. You can only make out the babies' skulls, they fit in the palm of your hand. But what I can tell you is that your father isn't here, his bones are still up there where he lived, at Gihanga, but don't you go looking for them, they're someplace where you shouldn't see them. All right, let's go now, you don't have to write anything in the book, that book's for the Bazungu, the white people, assuming they'll come, or for the grand gentlemen from Kigali in their four-by-fours. There's nothing for you to write, you're on the side of the dead. But let me tell you again, don't go looking for your father's remains, you mustn't see him where they left him."

She stepped over the back courtyard's broken fence and found herself in another banana grove, which seemed more overgrown than the one she'd just come through. Even with the weeds, she could make out a path. It led to a thicket that exuded a horrible stench, veiled by a buzzing, humming fog of mosquitoes, gnats, and fat green flies. A black puddle had overflowed and spread all around it, like stinking lava. Pallid, almost transparent worms twisted and writhed wherever the flood hadn't yet dried to a sickening crust.

She forced her way through the tall grass and sat down for a moment on the termite mound where people used to wait their turn every morning. The smell was almost more than she could bear, the air felt thick and heavy. She wasn't sure she could go on, wasn't sure she had the courage to climb the last few meters to that putrid thicket. But she told herself that she had to see this through to the end, that in just a few steps her journey would be over. She staggered up the last slope, tried to whisk away the blinding mist of gnats, and bent over the side of the latrine. She thought she could see something shaped like a human body in the filth, and maybe – but surely this was an illusion – the horrible black glistening of what used to be a face. A violent nausea washed over her, and she vomited as she ran back to the termite mound. She closed her eyes, only to see once again what she'd just glimpsed in the latrine, that same fleshless face in its vile, viscous mask. She opened her eyes to make that vision of horror go away. She was sure she would never again close her eyes without that monstrous face appearing from the deepest darkness. She ran down the hill and took shelter among the crumbling walls of Népomucène's cabaret, close by the roadside. To keep from closing her eyes, she stared at a bamboo rack, still dotted with a few clods of red clay. Trembling with fever and racked by nausea, she sat there for hours, watching for the truck to come back, like a promise of deliverance.

All night long she struggled against sleep in the room she'd rented at the mission, trying to hold back the flood of visions and nightmares that would sweep her into their world of terror if she let herself drift off for even a moment. Pitch darkness submerged the mission when the curfew hour came and the generator was turned off. She saw the glow of a fire through the narrow window: the watchmen warming themselves on this cold, dry-season night. She wished she could join them, hold out her hands toward the flames, talk with the men. But of course a girl couldn't mingle with strangers in the middle of the night. She remembered that she'd seen a hurricane lamp on the little table, and surely a box of matches next to it. She felt around for the matches, struck one, and lit the lamp's wick. It felt like that trembling, blue-tipped flame was watching over her, keeping at bay the dark forces that lurked all around. She lay down on the bed and finally fell into a dreamless sleep.

There was someone in her room when she awoke. In the dim early morning light, she recognized the guard from the church, sitting in the room's only chair.

"You went to your old house in Gihanga," said the old man. "Don't tell me what you saw or thought you saw there. You went right through to the end, there's nothing beyond it, and no way out of it. You won't find your dead in the graves or the bones or the latrine. That's not where they're waiting for you. They're inside you. They only survive in you, and you only survive through them. But from now on you'll find all your strength in them, there's no other choice, and no one can take that strength away from you. With that strength you can do things you might not even imagine today. Like it or not, the death of our loved ones has fueled us – not with hate, not with vengefulness, but with an energy that nothing can ever defeat. That strength lives in you too, don't let anyone try to tell you to get over your loss, not if that means saying goodbye to your dead. You can't: they'll never leave you, they stay by your side to give you the courage to live, to triumph over obstacles, whether here in Rwanda or abroad, if you go back. They're always beside you, and you can always depend on them."

Now the rising sun was lighting her tiny room. She sat on the edge of the bed, elbows on her knees, head in her hands, listening. She let the guardian's words sink into her, and little by little despair loosened its grip.

They sat for a long while looking at each other in silence. Her visitor picked up a little gourd that he'd set down at his feet. He dropped a single straw into it:

"I made this sorghum beer for the dead I watch over," he said. "Share it with them as I do."

He handed her the straw and she sucked up the liquid. She closed her eyes. A gentle bitterness filled her mouth, like something she'd felt long before.

"Now," said the guardian of the dead, "what is there for you to fear?"

archipelago books

is a not-for-profit literary press devoted to
promoting cross-cultural exchange through innovative
classic and contemporary international literature
www.archipelagobooks.org